Hundreds of Stanley Wilson's short stories, articles and photographs have appeared in magazines and newspapers throughout the United Kingdom and overseas. Many of the stories have been broadcast by the British Broadcasting Corporation, New Zealand Broadcasting Corporation, South African Broadcasting Corporation, British Forces Broadcasting Service, Capital Radio and Radio Telefis Eireann.

Past chairman of the Writer's Summer School, Swanwick, he regularly conducts courses and discussions on various aspects of writing at the School and at writers' gatherings elsewhere. He lectures on creative writing in general and on short story writing in particular. He has given talks on radio and has presented a series on BBC Radio York. For Alan Ayckbourn, at Scarborough's Stephen Joseph Theatre-in-the-Round, he was editor of a weekly cabaret-style show, 'Scarborough Airings'.

THE WAY OF THE SEA
and other stories

Every story in this collection was written by Stanley Wilson with radio in mind. The BBC has broadcast all of them, and many have been used overseas. All have appeared in magazines or newspapers. The stories range the globe and beyond, from India to Canadian backwoods, from an expedition up the Amazon to a hundred years' journey to the planet Eithnan, from the Caribbean to a rain-sodden English seaside promenade, and from a fishing trawler to a hospital ward. There is frustration, there is tenderness, there is horror, there are tears, but there is laughter as well.

STANLEY WILSON

THE WAY OF THE SEA

and other stories

Complete and Unabridged

ULVERSCROFT
Leicester

First published in Great Britain

First Large Print Edition
published 1999

British Library CIP Data

Wilson, Stanley, *1915–*
   The way of the sea and other stories.
   —Large print ed.—
   Ulverscroft large print series: general fiction
   1. Large type books
   I. Title
   823.9'14 [F]

   ISBN 0–7089–4065–X

Published by
F. A. Thorpe (Publishing) Ltd.
Anstey, Leicestershire
Set by Words & Graphics Ltd.
Anstey, Leicestershire
Printed and bound in Great Britain by
T. J. International Ltd., Padstow, Cornwall

This book is printed on acid-free paper

Dedicated to AUDREY

Foreword

Every story in this collection was written with radio in mind. The BBC has broadcast all of them, and repeated several, either on the national network or on local radio. Many have been similarly used by New Zealand Broadcasting Corporation, South African Broadcasting Corporation, Radio Telefís Eireann, British Forces Broadcasting Service and Capital Radio. Several were sold for worldwide use in the BBC's Transcription Service. All have appeared in magazines or newspapers in Britain and overseas.

The writing leans intentionally towards a conversational style, perhaps displeasing to the strict grammarian but welcomed by the listener in the kitchen, the patient in a hospital bed, the driver on a motorway and the expatriate in Holland. Coupled with first person narration, the aim is to create an atmosphere of intimacy where precise compliance with syntax might fail to produce the desired effect.

Most of the stories have a story about themselves. For example, the announcer of 'This Side of Heaven', written as a tearjerker, may not have been weeping when the broadcast ended but there was a brief silence before she said, a noticeable catch in her voice, 'That story was written by . . . '. 'The Birthday' (originally 'The Fab, Fab Day'), however, was responsible for at least one flood of tears. The broadcast was barely over when an acquaintance, two hundred miles away, reaching for yet another handkerchief, telephoned to say, through intermittent sobs, how greatly she had enjoyed the tale.

Other stories such as 'The Memories Man', 'The Masterpiece' and 'Gone all Native' were written with horror very much in mind. A producer at BBC Radio York shuddered after his preliminary reading of 'Gone all Native' and agreed to broadcast it only after much persuasion. Capital Radio, however, entertained no such qualms about using it in the 'Moment of Terror' series.

A most satisfying, but not evident, relationship exists between 'The Sand of Karilaa' and 'Camel of Zayid'. Both were published in 'The Yorkshire Evening Post', both are set in the Middle East and both were read on BBC radio, a gap of twenty-five years between. The reader on each occasion was that master of accents, Garrard Green. New Zealand Broadcasting Corporation used 'The Sand of Karilaa' and it was a runner-up in a BBC Pebble Mill travel-story competition. 'Camel of Zayid', broadcast by the British Forces Broadcasting Service from Malta and printed again in Britain and overseas, has proved to be the most popular story in this collection. Following its BBC broadcast there were numerous requests for copies of the script, including calls from libraries and from listeners in Holland and France.

'The Way of the Sea' was originally submitted to London's now defunct 'Evening News'. The fiction editor did not find the ending acceptable. The BBC, however, was thoroughly satisfied with it. Read by the actress, Brenda Bruce, the tale was broadcast twice in a fortnight and it appeared subsequently in a monthly magazine. The version in the present collection is twice the length of the original broadcast: the theme and the characters seemed to merit treatment of greater depth. The plot, because of the slowly mounting conflict, also seemed well suited to attenuation.

The lengths of many of the other tales have been reduced by excising the repetition introduced originally for the sake of emphasis. While the reader of the printed word can refer to an earlier paragraph for elucidation, the radio listener can never back-track. Once uttered, the words disappear into the ether for ever. So it is often wise in radio writing to repeat, in paraphrase, some salient point. Furthermore many authors, re-reading their work after an interval, make changes and thus, they hope, effect improvement. Every item in this collection was scrutinised and pruned with this in view.

One character, James Clancy, appears in several stories. Irish master mariner Clancy revelled in a series of battles with the resident customs officer at an obscure port a few miles south of Dublin. He was victorious in every confrontation except the last. For one listener at least Clancy will always be real. Never, she says, can she take a stroll along Dublin's O'Connell Street without the hope of catching sight of an exaggerated rolling gait that so typified the boastful, belly-laughing Cap'n Jimmy Clancy.

Apart from their appearance in print and on the air, all the stories in the collection have been recorded for use by Bristol's 'Avon Talking Magazine for the Blind'. Two of them, both Clancy tales, after broadcast by South African Broadcasting Corporation, were taken by the library of 'Tape Aids for the Blind' in Johannesburg.

Contents

The Way of the Sea

She hadn't noticed him. He was seated on an upturned fish box in the corner of the baiting shed, impaling mussels on the hooks spaced along the nylon fishing line.

'Hi, toothsome!'

She paused, half interested, half revolted, to watch the deftness of his thick spatulate fingers, pincering a mussel and thrusting the oozing flesh on to a barbed hook.

Her tone was guarded.

'Morning!'

Quickly she walked away.

He leapt from the baiting shed and at once barred her path. She glanced quickly to right and to left. There was no easy escape. The path between the mountain of carelessly piled fish boxes and the maze of taut mooring ropes was not only narrow but, strewn with the remains of fish guts from the morning catches spurned by the seagulls, hazardous as well.

'I — I beg your pardon!' she said, struggling to sound imperious.

He was jovial, impudent.

'Scared you? Didn't mean to. Don't often

1

come across 'em like you round here,' he said.

She assessed the stained woollen jersey, the huge yet handsome hands, slimy from their encounter with a thousand mussels, the ruddy complexion, the stubble far more than one day's growth.

'Like — like me?!'

At the risk of snagging her tights on the corner of a fish box she attempted to sidestep.

He sidestepped too.

'I'm not aiming to eat you. Fancy you, though, in another way!'

'How dare . . . ?!'

His tone was bantering.

'Aw, c'mon, c'mon, woman!'

Seeking escape, she glanced up and down the quay. It was mid-day. The morning fish auction finished, fishermen, salesmen and buyers all gone. Nor were there any other holidaymakers. Her jaw, set firm, failed to conceal her nervousness.

'Would you mind . . . ?!'

'Mind what?'

'Stepping aside!'

'And let you go?!'

'At once!'

'Not until you've told me all about yourself.'

'What d'you want?'

'You!'

'Me?!'

'A visitor?'

'Yes.'

'Where from?'

'Mind your own business. Now, are you going to let me . . . ?'

'Okay. You're a visitor. By the accent — Leeds. Right? — Oh, stop all that backing off. Look out, look out. That pile of boxes!'

A stack of fish boxes seemed about to topple. He thrust out a protective hand.

She shrank away.

'Don't — don't you dare touch . . . '

His eye slowly appraised her, from the white sling-back shoes to her jet black hair.

'If you'd brought that lot down I'd've been forced to touch you. Pick you up, in fact!'

She was trembling, her voice high.

'Get, get . . . '

He shrugged and dropped the hand that had remained poised in mid-air.

'Okay, okay!'

Smiling, shrugging, he stepped to one side. She darted past him and fled to the far end of the fish quay. At its junction with the promenade she paused, gasping. She turned. He was following. In spite of the rubber thigh boots, their tops loosely flopping about his knees, his gait was measured, confident.

He held out both arms as if in supplication.

'Sorry!' he called, 'I didn't mean to put the wind up you.'

She swallowed hard and began to make her urgent way along the promenade. He caught up and fell into step.

'See you this evening?'

She did not reply. They crossed the road to Mariner Steps.

As she began to climb he bounded ahead, taking the worn sandstone steps three at a time to swing round and bar her way. There was now not the faintest vestige of banter in his tone. It was curiously childlike in its earnestness.

'I — I'm sorry. Dunno what came over me. Please. This evening. Will you?' He was panting. 'Sevenish, down here?'

Without a word she slipped past the bulky frame and continued up the steps.

This time he did not follow.

At the top she turned into Mariner Row. Breathless from the climb, she paused to fling a brief glance over her shoulder. He was standing where she had left him. He raised seven fingers.

'Yes?' he called.

'No, no!' she mouthed, shaking her head, 'No!'

4

She let herself into the holiday flat, at once hurried to the window and managed to catch a glimpse of him as he turned to retrace his steps to the promenade.

At three o'clock, the meal, perfunctorily prepared at one o'clock, still lay on the table, scarcely touched. She drank coffee, more coffee. She switched on and switched off the television set half-a-dozen times in as many minutes. The radio equally offered no comforting escape. At intervals throughout that afternoon she sought the window with its uninterrupted view of Mariner Steps and a section of the promenade far below.

Four o'clock. Her bath was a leisurely indulgence. Five o'clock. She began to dress, slowly and with infinite care. She moved from room to room, mirror to mirror, tending her hair there and there, her make-up there and there and there. Earrings examined and discarded, bracelets slipped on then dragged off, necklaces subjected to a scrutiny unknown since the day they were selected over a jeweller's counter, a solitaire diamond ring, worn almost daily for the past five years, diplomatically laid aside.

Six-fifty-five. She stepped quickly out of the door. An onlooker, close at hand, might have glimpsed a faint tremble in the fingers that turned the key. But there were no onlookers. Mariner Row that April evening was deserted.

★ ★ ★

They met at the foot of Mariner Steps.

'Phew. Luscious!' he said.

She smiled. There was not even a whisper of fear in her now, nothing but an elation that she made little effort to conceal. Gone were his navy blue woollen jersey, the jeans and the rubber thigh boots. He was immaculate now in dark pin-stripe suit and white shirt. The days'-old stubble gone, the hands now betrayed nothing of their morning occupation.

'Your wife turns you out rather sharpish,' she said.

'What wife?!'

Her expression was one of surprise bordering on pleasure.

'Sorry. I thought . . . '

'Well, you were wrong.'

'And haven't you ever . . . ?'

'Been churched? — No, if that's what you mean!'

'Well, I'd've thought . . . '

He shrugged.

'They've come and they've gone.'

'And what plans have you got for me?' she said lightly.

They had strolled to the end of the promenade, to the point where it became a narrow footway between the rocks that ringed much of Cragwick Bay, before he replied.

'Permanent!' he said.

'P-permanent?!'

'D'you take a drink?' he said without looking at her.

'Now and again.'

His hand rested lightly on her arm, a contact she made no effort to break as they strolled in silence back to Mariner Steps.

'A path about halfway up to the left,' he said, 'takes us to the Mariner's Arms.'

Customers in the bar were few. All were abruptly silent as he ushered her through the door. He nodded to them in perfunctory fashion and steered her towards the snug. Conscious of their stares, she quickened her pace.

'Friends of yours?' she said as she took the proffered chair in the otherwise deserted room.

'Fishermen, all of them. Same as me.'

'They seemed highly interested.'

'In you, yes. Show me a feller who wouldn't be.'

The flattery clearly pleased. She laughed. 'Nonsense!'

'I'm telling you. Only in summer do they ever come across women like yourself. Even then not all that many. But, what with pleasure-boating and round-the-bay fishing trips, they're all too busy to bother. What's it to be?'

'Dry sherry, please.'

He returned from the serving hatch with a pint of beer, a glass of rum and a schooner of sherry.

Eyebrows high, she said, 'You, all that?'

He laughed.

'On special occasions, yes.'

'Is this special?'

'Hoping,' he said softly, 'hoping!'

She sipped at her glass.

'Always been a fisherman?'

'Yes.'

'You don't talk like one.'

'My mother nursed a lot of fancy ideas about me and my future, never letting me forget she'd married beneath her, a common fisherman. I drifted.' He had already consumed his beer. At a single gulp he emptied the glass of rum. 'Another?'

She drained her sherry glass.

'No thanks.'

'Let's go then.'

He took her arm and hurried her through the bar. The same men were still there. Conversation died the moment that the pair appeared.

'Goodnight!' he flung back over his shoulder.

'Night!'

Arm encircling her waist, he hastened her up Mariner Steps and across Mariner Row to the holiday flat. She made to slide the key into the lock. His hand clamped over hers as if to consume it. He slammed the door behind them and seized her in an embrace that made her gasp.

His voice was tense, the words scarcely audible.

'I want you, woman. Going mad for you!'

'No, no, please . . .'

'Which door?' he whispered hoarsely.

He picked her up and carried her into the living room. She struggled desperately to free herself.

His kiss was smothering, long sustained and violent.

'I'm taking you, woman — now and for always.'

She began to shiver. Uncontrollably. He held her in a vice-like embrace.

'Please. No, no. — Oh . . . '

They coupled in silence, wildly, briefly, and when it was over his hands for idle minutes strayed up and down her naked back.

Then, 'You're everything I imagined you'd be. Everything,' he said softly as he got to his feet.

'Don't — don't go. Please!' she whispered.

★ ★ ★

'Miraculous!' her sister said when she arrived home in Leeds. 'Told you, didn't I, the seaside even in April was the best pick-me-up? Never seen you looking so well. Absolutely blooming!'

She smiled and, after supper, she told her sister about him.

'You — you stupid, irresponsible bitch. Picked up by a common fisherman? The sooner you forget about him the better. Unless, of course you've come home with a little keepsake in prospect.'

'I wouldn't mind!'

'You wouldn't . . . '

'He wants me to marry him!'

'Now, I've heard the lot. You of all women. For years fending 'em off. Then nabbed and bedded in a couple of weeks.'

10

'In a day!'

'What do you mean?!!'

'It happened the same day.'

The sister stared at her, open-mouthed.

'You? Never! Remember, after Nigel, how you swore next time it'd have to be a man who didn't urge you to bed within minutes of meeting him? He'd need to have a good family, a sound education. And dripping with money, bursting with old world courtesy. And now throwing yourself at a penniless ignorant fisherman with all the graces of a sea-front winkle stall!'

She laughed.

'No, no, no! How wrong can you get? — Does this mean you won't be coming to the wedding?'

'Wedding?!'

'Next month. Before he gets too busy. Fishing's hectic in summer.'

'Have you gone completely mad? A brief, passionate flirtation — I can accept that — but marriage!'

'Are you coming to the wedding?!'

'Not likely!'

★ ★ ★

By noon next day she had emptied her wardrobe, cleared every drawer in the bedroom. By teatime everything had been packed.

Throughout they had studiously avoided each other. Late that evening there was confrontation on the stairs.

'Still determined?!'

'Completely.'

She retraced her steps to the bedroom and began to write address labels for the suitcases. Her sister had followed.

'What's it like, this — this 'Pebble Cottage'?'

She paused, pen in air, to glance at the precisely gardened, run-of-the-mill semi-detached house on the opposite side of the road.

'Detached, a dream of a spot, informal, charming, brimming with character.'

'A view of the sea?'

'Step out of the door and the whole of Cragwick beach for a front garden.'

'A decent bathroom? — You know what you're like with bathrooms!'

She ignored the question as she gathered together the suitcases. Arms akimbo, the sister stepped in front of her.

'The bathroom, is it all right?'

'Yes.'

'Just 'yes'?'

She frowned.

'I mean what I say — 'yes'. I've — I've told you enough.'

★ ★ ★

It was idyllic, her first Cragwick summer. He was attentive, amorous, excessively so, yet frantically acceptable. They were sufficient to themselves.

Each morning, after dragging his coble single-handed down the slipway, he put to sea at five o'clock, always on his own. The rest of the fishermen at Cragwick sailed in pairs.

He was invariably the first off, jealously guarding details of where precisely he dropped his pots or laid his lines. And he was always ahead of the rest in making harbour late afternoon, always the first to unload the catch of lobsters and crabs or, according to season, haddock, plaice and cod.

The pair became a standing joke in the bar of the Mariner's Arms.

'And still got strength to haul up the catch on his own!'

His appetite for her was insatiable, taking her the moment he stepped across the threshold of Pebble Cottage, the moment they climbed into bed at night and often at the hazy moment of early morning between sleeping and waking. She almost surprised herself — she would have amazed and astonished her sister — that the lingering and ineradicable odours of fish guts and diesel oil never once stemmed the flood of her own appetite.

★ ★ ★

The joys of loving in Pebble Cottage continued but the idyll of living there was too soon rudely shattered.

It was late November. He had put to sea early as usual. The tides of November far exceeded predictions. Lashed by a pitiless north-easter, they reached the very walls of Pebble Cottage. Mid-morning she retreated, terrified, to a corner of the scullery at the back of the cottage. Sea water, in spite of a barricade of sandbags, spurted under the front door and gurgled resentfully as it receded.

She screamed in abject terror as the chimney stack crashed through the cottage's pantiled roof, holing their bedroom ceiling and floor, scattering bricks and mortar across the living room.

He was home by noon, fishing trip abandoned. He had found it impossible to launch the coble. Towards midnight the gale subsided and together they succeeded in covering the gaping hole in the cottage's roof with a tarpaulin.

She wept as they struggled to lift sodden carpets and drag them to the jumble of high rocks behind the cottage.

'I can't — I daren't go on living here, alone day after day, love. I'm terrified.'

He took her in his arms.

'Don't worry. I'll do something.'

* * *

It was approaching spring when at last they moved. To a terrace house halfway up Main Street, safer, if not entirely safe, from November gales but hemmed in by neighbours. From the outset she loathed it.

'There's nothing else in the village, nothing. This'll have to do us for now,' he said as they got into bed the first night in that terrace house.

She was less than generous.

'What's up?' he said.

'This room. I feel as though we're on view, as though the neighbours there and there and there are all listening and watching!'

He was annoyed, frustrated.

'Don't be so damn stupid, woman!'
She turned her back on him and went to sleep.

* * *

It was an evening in April when he first struck her. He had returned from sea late afternoon and, as usual, they made love. As they lay together afterwards, his fingers lightly caressing her naked stomach, he said, 'No sign of a youngster yet?'

She was silent.

His open palm pressed on her navel.

'No youngsters, hm?!'

' 'Fraid not.'

'What's wrong with you?' he said.

'So far as I know — not a thing.'

'Then why . . . ?'

She spoke slowly, wistfully.

'I don't know. I just do not know. I wonder if it could be . . . '

She paused and laid her hand on his.

'Could be what?' he said idly.

'Perhaps your fault, not mine!'

He leapt up to tower over her, menacing.

'You what?!'

Her voice was soft.

'Well, it could be. It has been known.'

The force of the blow on her cheek drove

her halfway off the bed. She put out a hand to avoid tumbling to the floor.

'And there's more where that came from — if ever you dare suggest a thing like that again, saucy bitch!'

She snatched up her clothes and, sobbing, tore downstairs where she quickly dressed. He followed.

'Next time, if ever there is a next time, I'll flay you, flay you!' he said as he stormed out of the house.

It was eleven o'clock when he returned, so drunk that she had to help him climb the stairs, far too drunk for any late-night lovemaking.

But by four o'clock next morning he was astir.

'Breakfast, woman!'

'What?' she murmured sleepily.

'Breakfast, quick!'

'Y-you mean . . . ?'

Instantly wide awake, she stared up at him, utterly without comprehension.

Ever since their wedding day he had brought her morning tea to the bedroom before preparing his own breakfast. He would willingly have packed his own sandwich box for his trip to sea but this she insisted upon attending to the night before.

'It's about time you did a bit of graft for

your corn. Over twelve months I've been carrying you.'

She dressed quickly.

'Better put some extras on,' he went on, 'or you'll freeze to death.'

Arms thrusting into a jumper she said, 'Freeze?'

'At the harbour. While I'm eating my breakfast you can take the sandwich box to the slipway, stow it aboard and check the lines and pots.'

She paused in her dressing.

'It's — it's still dark!'

He sneered.

'What're you scared about? Nobody's going to touch you. And if they did — well, they'd leave nowt behind.'

'I don't know what you . . . '

'Mean? I mean if some guy happened to rape you, nothing'd happen later!'

She began to sob.

'Oh, shurrup, woman!'

The blow pitched her against the wardrobe. Hand to her cheek, she screamed. He grabbed her by the shoulders, swung her round and marched her down the stairs.

'All — all this because I haven't given you a child so far?'

'Breakfast. Then to the harbour — quick!'

Dawn was streaking the night sky when

18

she reached the fishing coble. She retched as she stepped over the gunwale on to the wet boards. In spite of raids by ravenous seagulls, remnants of fish guts lay scattered here and there. The stench of oil fumes lay heavy in the bottom of the craft.

She stowed the sandwich box in the locker of the coble, made a perfunctory inspection of the lobster pots and lines then made her way back along the jetty. Pursued by wolf whistles from other fishermen now gathering, she took to her heels and did not slacken pace until, panting and exhausted, she reached the house in Main Street.

He was about to leave.

'Taken your time, haven't you?'

Still panting, she said, 'Fast — fast as I could manage.' And, as if to placate him, 'I hope everything's all right!'

'It'd better be. I've been thinking,' he said. 'I mentioned earning your corn, remember?'

'Y-yes.'

'Plenty of jobs coming up this summer. Dish-washing in the cafés, cleaning up in the boarding houses.'

Horror seized her.

'But I couldn't . . .'

'But you will,' he flung back at her as the door closed behind him.

19

She took a job, a whole series of jobs, mostly in guest houses: dusting, polishing, changing bed-linen on Saturday mornings in readiness for the next batch of holidaymakers.

Her working day began after preparing his breakfast and tending his fishing coble.

It continued with carrying bulging suitcases to upper floors and ended under a torrent of abuse from her husband for not having supper ready the moment that he arrived home from his day's fishing.

Then her sister came from Leeds.

'I might have known. What a dump. Just look at the state of your hands, your hair, your skin, your clothes. In all these years I've never . . . You're coming home with me, dear. Start afresh!'

'But my job there . . . '

'Plenty of others, plenty. What time does he get himself in?'

She glanced at the clock.

'Another couple of hours at least.'

'Plenty of time to pack then!'

Two days later he followed the pair to Leeds. He burst through the front door, leaving it wide open.

'Where the hell are you?'

She appeared at the top of the staircase.

'What — what do you want?'

'Bloody daft question. Down. Or do I have to drag you?'

The sister rushed from the kitchen.

'How dare you? Bursting into my house like this?'

The front door still lay wide open. She was respectable semi-detached, desperately anxious to stay that way. The neighbours might see and hear.

'We can talk in there,' she said hurriedly, pointing towards the living room.

'Talk? Who wants to talk? Out of the way,' he said. 'You've made enough trouble already. — Now, you up there. If you're not down in ten seconds I'll be up and drag you down. I'm not wasting any more time. A whole day's fishing lost already.'

★ ★ ★

Back at the terrace house in Cragwick's Main Street he bundled her through the front door and at once began to beat her. Beat her until he was weary and breathless.

For days on end she could not speak, she could barely whimper. She flinched whenever he came near her. And she screamed and clawed his face whenever he attempted to take her.

Because of the bruises on her face and her arms, because of the blackened eyes and swollen lips it was a fortnight before she could summon up sufficient courage to stumble as far as the shop on the corner of Mariner Row, and even then only with a shawl over her head.

The woman in the shop was warm and understanding and sympathetic. She already knew a great deal about him and her.

'You'd be a damn sight better off without him, love!'

'Without him? I've tried. I went. He dragged me back. It was hell. I couldn't face . . .'

'That's only one way of getting rid. There's many another. Many and many another.'

He arrived home from sea earlier than expected that day. So far she had given little thought to preparing his evening meal. He stumped into the scullery where she was bathing her bruises with cold water.

'What about food?!' he bellowed. 'Nowt much going on here, is there?'

She followed as he tore back into the living room.

'W-what's the matter?!'

He dragged off his thigh boots, hurled one at the bare table and the other in her direction. She doubled up with a shriek as the heavy boot caught her squarely in the stomach.

'Empty table, empty useless belly!' he roared.

She fled to the scullery.

'I'm — I'm sorry, sorry,' she gasped.

★ ★ ★

The woman at the corner shop next morning said, 'I'm amazed nobody warned you. He's notorious. Always has been, always a brute. Arrogant, an absolute fiend with women.'

'But he was so . . . .'

'Yes, yes, I know. So attentive, so pressing, so attractive, so generous. One girl I knew couldn't stand it a minute longer. They found her on the rocks at low water.'

'Found . . . ?'

'Dead. Drowned.'

'Not him, surely?!'

'Not exactly. Suicide. But he drove her to it. And gets off, of course, scot free. He's a killer!'

The shop woman, a wary eye on the door, edged round the counter.

'And you could be!'

'I could be what?'

'A killer. In fact I think you'll have to be.'

'Oh, no, no . . . '

The woman edged closer.

'Not even if you could never, never be found out?!'

The shopkeeper thrust a small mirror into her hand.

'Take a good look at yourself. How much longer will you put up with it? You don't need to. Not for another single day. Would you like to know more?'

'No, no, I — I couldn't.'

The woman threw up both hands.

Her tone was dismissive.

'Better him than you.'

'What d'you mean?'

'He'll break you. Only a matter of weeks. Mark my words.'

'Oh, I couldn't, I couldn't!'

She drew a limp hand across her brow, then withdrew it to contemplate her open palm. It was wet.

'You could. And you may have to. Listen to me!' the shopwoman said.

'All right — go on. — But I don't promise . . . '

* * *

Because his breakfast next morning was not waiting for him fifteen minutes after he had

24

thrust her out of the bed, he slapped her face and told her to get the hell out of it to that sister of hers in Leeds.

But she had not gone to her sister. In the middle of the morning she spent a whole hour talking to the woman at the corner shop.

★ ★ ★

'Still here?' he said, not wholly without humour as he stepped into the house that evening. 'Prefer me to your sister, then?'

She was in the scullery so he was unaware of an expression on her face that wholly belied the lightly-voiced reply, 'I couldn't possibly leave, could I, all that steak and kidney ready for making into a pie for you!'

They ate in silence.

'Not a bad pint of ale,' he said, after his second helping of steak and kidney pudding, and a third tankard of beer. He had not noticed that she had eaten barely at all. 'Quite a treat. Come into money?'

'I'd put away a pound or two after that last café job,' she said.

'Glad to see you spending in the right direction!'

He had fallen asleep, as usual, in a fireside

chair by the time she had cleared the table and washed up. With his sandwich box, a pad saw and a drill, a chisel, a hammer and some nails, and a tin containing tar, she crept out of the house. She scurried down Main Street in the direction of the slipway, now deserted. His fishing coble was only just discernible in the deepening gloom.

Laboriously hacking out a section of the planking concealed by the locker in the bows of the craft, she nailed the section to the bottom of the sandwich box. Then, lacing its edges liberally with tar, she rammed it back into place.

Somewhere in the lee of Black Horse Rock — at that particular period, his favourite fishing spot — after sliding crab and lobster pots overside he would drop anchor to settle down to eat his sandwiches then drift off to sleep. At first the sandwich box would refuse to budge. He would curse and lunge and drag at it. Then, one final jerk, it should come away, and ten fathoms of sea water surge through the hole she had made in the hull.

Of course, he would battle like a fiend to bale out. For ten or, at the most, fifteen minutes, the woman in the corner shop had reckoned.

They would find him, eventually. But there would never be any trace of the coble, ten fathoms down on the bed of the sea.

★ ★ ★

Next morning she left him as he ate breakfast to make her daily trek to the slipway. The cardboard carton supplied by the shopkeeper tucked under her coat looked exactly like his sandwich box.

'Rain in the air, I think,' she said, tapping the bulge. 'Better keep your sandwiches well covered!'

She glanced about her. The slipway was deserted. She pitched the box into the waters of the harbour and watched it fill with water and sink.

He was about to leave when she returned to the house. She kissed him, lightly. He sneered. And the sudden faint pangs of remorse died almost before they could draw breath. But he returned the kiss, roughly, and he slapped her ruthlessly across the backside.

She sat before the fire in silence. At noon the remains of breakfast still lay on the table. The tap over the sink had been dripping steadily since early morning.

Two o'clock. In three hours' time

he — it — could begin to drift southwards on the tide from the north. It might be picked up on the rocks at the end of the promenade tomorrow, next week, next month . . . She had not lived in Cragwick very long but she had been there long enough to know something about the way of the sea.

Five o'clock. She sprang from her chair. She washed and put on her best frock. In front of the mirror she devoted an hour to brushing her hair and then applying make-up to conceal the bruise on her cheek-bone.

She began to pack. Her eyes strayed to the window and a glimpse of the sea. The tide was lapping gently up the empty slipway. She watched. A solitary vessel rounded the headland. Her husband's coble was invariably the first home. But there were two men, not just one, in the returning craft.

She resumed her packing. Ten minutes and she glanced again towards the slipway. The fishermen were tying up their cobles. There was no sign of her husband.

Quickly she put on a coat and opened her purse. Shaking her head she tipped the coins on the table and counted them twice. She frowned.

'Damn! Another ten pounds at least!?' she muttered.

Then she stiffened. There was the unmistakable sound of heavy thigh-boots pounding the pavement.

'Oh, no, no!'

Both hands sought her half-open mouth. She waited for him to burst in. There was a gentle knock. She stepped forward and gingerly opened the door. A fisherman stood on the threshold, holding a basket of struggling lobsters. There was a wound on his face. The blood had caked.

Her voice was piping.

'What — what d'you want?'

'Something to tell you,' the man said. 'There was a scrap.'

She gripped the edge of the door.

'A scrap?!'

'A fight. Me and him. I dropped my pots, same as his, yon side of Black Horse.'

'Go on, go on.' She glanced swiftly up and down the street. 'No, no, come inside, quick!'

She seized the man by the arm and she dragged him into the room.

'Well, go on, go on!'

'It were like this . . . '

'Yes, yes . . . '

'We lost his coble. Sprung a leak the minute we got her in tow. — You'll get along all right without him, missus. — I daresay a woman like yourself'll get wed again pretty quick.'

She thumped the table. The coins lying there jumped in protest.

'Tell me, tell me, you fool. — What happened?!'

'Seconds and it was all over.'

'What . . . ? Go on, go on!'

'He were bloody mad, me dropping pots near his. He shot up, grabbed the spare anchor and swung at me.'

His fingers went to the left side of his face, to the wound that slashed the flesh from ear-lobe to mouth-corner. Instinctively her hand went to caress the hidden bruise on her own cheek.

'Then what?'

'The cobles barely a yard apart. A bit of a swell. — You get it both ways near Black Horse . . . '

'And, and, and . . . ?'

'The anchor rope must've tangled round his legs. Just too late when we got him hauled aboard.'

'Too late?!'

She laughed, she screamed. The man made to place a hand on her arm. She hurled him aside.

'Don't — don't take on so, missus. An accident, I swear.'

He pointed to the lobsters.

'Them's his.'

'His? Take them, I don't want them. Get them out of here!'

The man shrugged and, picking up the basket, turned towards the door.

'An accident, honest, missus.'

Suddenly calm, she stepped forward to bar his way. She threw a brief glance at the coins, the contents of her purse, scattered over the table.

'Did — did you say they were his lobsters?'

The man nodded.

'Get me ten pounds for them!'

'Ten? They're worth forty, nay, fifty of anybody's money.'

'A ten pound note!' she said firmly.

The man stared, bewildered.

'But . . .'

'Go on, get me ten!'

The man thrust a hand under his woollen jersey, dragged out some notes and placed one of them on the table.

And he had scarcely gone past the window on his way down Main Street when she picked up her case, and the money, for that journey to her sister in Leeds.

The Other Experiment

Precisely how long we had stood and waited in the reception area of the planet Eithnan I could neither calculate nor did I care. I was young once more and, Magdala at my side, blissfully content.

The exquisite Magdala had been my own discovery.

'Scour the earth for the perfect partner,' Wilkins said the day I was selected for the crew of the Eithnan project. 'Don't get trapped by milk-white teeth, violet eyes and vital statistics.'

'At my stage in life? You must be joking!'

'One foot in the grave yet vital statistics can still appeal! First and foremost go for intellect. Choose with the most infinite care. She's likely to be with you for, shall we say, quite some time — if we can talk in terms of time as we know it on earth. Reject anybody less than two hundred and fifty cephadiolons.'

'Two-fifty? — At his peak Einstein barely nudged one hundred!'

Wilkins laughed.

'Glad the message is getting through.'

I began the search. Five continents, a thousand suggested trails, all to nowhere.

Then I chanced upon a minute island off the east African coast. Long before we touched down, the chatter of my cephadioloscope had soared to a scream. It latched unerringly on a jungle clearing and there a half-naked crone, skin like tree bark, eyes all but hidden by lids dry as dead leaves.

Like a man in a frenzy, the cephadioloscope battled to escape from my grasp. I kept my distance from the loathsome creature that so strangely attracted the instrument. The stench from her was that of an open sewer in the heat of a tropical mid-day sun.

'I'm — er — I'm looking for somebody,' I said, striving to conceal my overwhelming revulsion.

The crone cackled.

'Me, Magdala!'

A claw-like finger stabbed at a pendulous, desiccated breast. My cephadioloscope continued to scream approval, its needle teetering at the three hundred mark.

The jungle creature flung back her head to laugh and I was staring, momentarily, into a cavern of blackened teeth.

'Y-you?!!'

The same claw-like finger thrust to within a millimetre of my eye.

'Decide upon what you wish to see — and you will see!'

A crackle now of static, a sudden lotus-eating warmth and I was back once more in the reception area of the planet Eithnan, Magdala still at my side, beautiful as a June dawn on distant Earth.

'You were a long way off,' she whispered.

'Dreaming. Back on Earth. An island off the coast of Africa. You there, a dried-up old hag. I've never been able to understand.'

Magdala's laugh was like the sound of clear, bright, trickling water.

'I had everything you were sent to find,' she said.

'Except beauty.'

'Your cephadioloscope wasn't programmed for trivia.'

'Yet now you are beautiful beyond all description,' I said, seeking her welcoming hand.

'Beautiful!' The word lingered on her lips. She made not the least effort to conceal her consummate joy. But then, with a venom more fitting to the tongue of a peevish old hag than that of an exquisite young woman, she added, 'May they never, never arrive!'

'But — but Magdala . . . '

'Remember what happened after we left that African island?' she said softly, all venom now evaporated.

'Not at all clearly.'

'The years of training for the flight, the steady, remorseless mind-purging of all earthly influences?'

'The only thing I can remember is you, darling!'

'Then I say it again. May they never, never arrive!'

'But just imagine,' I said, 'meeting Wilkins again after all these years!'

'If only it could be Wilkins. He is long gone.'

'If not Wilkins, then who?'

'It's ten earth-centuries since you and I landed here. The journey itself lasted ninety earth-years.'

'Ten centuries?!'

'Check the build-up of cosmic dust over the reception area. Our first job on landing, remember, to make this clearing. I estimate one millimetre depth of dust for every seventeen years since then.'

I stole a glance at Magdala: youthful, radiant, her eyes sparkling, complexion faultless. I shook my head in disbelief.

'But you look no more than twenty. Almost

eleven centuries? I can't believe . . . If we managed to survive why not Wilkins as well?'

'You and I, my love, are the experiment, Wilkins merely the experimenter. He had no hope of survival to witness the outcome of his work. That was something for his distant descendants. And the longer we wait the greater our hope of their failure!'

For the millionth time I scanned the vast and, as ever, blank reaches of the reception area.

'But surely, Magdala, meeting Wilkins or whoever after all this time could be a fantastic experience,' I said. 'Even before you and I left Earth their knowledge was near enough total.'

In one so radiantly young the smile was oddly mature, for an instant bordering on the patronising.

'Far from total,' Magdala said. 'Wilkins felt sure of one thing only. Without problems of food, water, oxygen and temperatures you and I would reach Eithnan and survive indefinitely. The rest was inspired guesswork. In eight or nine or, at the most, ten hundred years, he calculated, his successors would come up with all the answers.'

'But if they've failed?' I said.

'You and I left here on Eithnan for ever — together!'

'Do — do you think they will come?'

'I am certain.'

'And part us?'

'Without doubt.'

'Then we'll go — now!'

Again that smile on Magdala's lips, a smile suggesting the wisdom of the ages.

'And where could we go?'

'Where they never would find us.'

Magdala, on the verge of tears, shook her head.

'Remember the cephadioloscope on Earth eleven centuries ago?'

'Vaguely.'

'Well, their present instruments make it seem crude as a water-diviner's piece of twig. Nowhere in the cosmos is entirely safe for us. There can be no escape, my darling. They would hunt — look, look!'

In the saffron-tinted sky a blue light, no larger than a pin-prick, had appeared. Blue slowly changed to silver and the pin-prick assumed a diamond shape.

A crowd of Eithnanians surged forward. There was turmoil as the spacecraft touched down.

I seized hold of Magdala's hand, tense and icy-cold to my eager touch.

'Quick,' I said, 'we ought to be with the reception committee. Imagine, our own flesh and blood inside that spaceship . . . '

Magdala tried, but failed, to take her hand away.

'No, no, my love. We have so little time.'

'But think. One thousand years of new knowledge from Earth inside that silver diamond.'

There was infinite sadness in the voice of the incomparable Magdala.

'Do you still love me?!'

'You know I do,' I said.

'Then make the most of these last few moments, I beg you.'

I took the unhappy, resisting woman firmly in my arms and together we soared over the host of clamouring Eithnanians to land on the exit platform of the ship, alongside four men from planet Earth, each of them much the same as the Wilkins I remembered.

I thrust out a hand.

'Wilkins! Welcome!'

The men from earth ignored my greeting.

'Wilkins! Why . . . ?'

Enveloped by a reception committee the new arrivals were at once whisked out of sight.

I turned to Magdala, now sobbing.

'Why didn't they . . . ?'

'A brief respite at least.'

'What d'you mean? Come along. Inside!'
Magdala shrank from me.
'No, no, please . . . '
'Well, I must. **We** must!' I said and, taking firm hold of her wrist, I led her through the open door of the spacecraft.
'The end, my love,' she whispered between sobs. 'The end with no goodbyes.'
'I don't understand,' I said.
'Then look!'
Two creatures, their backs at first to us, began to turn. One a male, in his late fifties, greying, gaunt, tall. The other a leathery-skinned, half-naked crone.
The lids of their tight-closed eyes were fluttering. Magdala gasped.
'I begged you, darling, not to come. I remember so well the secrets of the African jungle. The zombies. Living creatures without life.'
I stole a glance at Magdala, beautiful beyond belief, then a glance at the crone, ugly and forbidding as a dead toad.
'Magdala, what . . . ?'
All at once she was serene, her touch on my arm like gossamer. A strange stillness and silence reigned.
Her voice, when it came, was soft, calm, almost chilling.
'When they despatched us from Earth

their experiment in suspended animation was barely beyond the embryo stage, with the aim of deep-freezing human beings for ultimate revival. Parallel with this there was the other experiment to separate the id, the mind, the intellect — call it what you will — from the body for eventual reunion.'

'Did they ever succeed?'

'With both. And to perfection. Wilkins was . . . look, look!'

The tall elderly man and the scrawny crone, the smell of death all around, were upon us.

Magdala screamed.

'The experiment over. We — now — go — back, my darling!'

The eyes of the gaunt man and the eyes of the desiccated crone had opened and were beginning to focus. On us.

'Magdala!'

I saw her, for what was to be the last time, in all her ethereal beauty. Steadily the features that I had adored for eleven centuries now began to darken and crumble.

'I admire Wilkins' work,' she said without emotion. 'Sad he derived no direct benefit. How fortunate his descendants, achieving their goal, suspended animation. This is how they survived the 90-year travel from Earth. And, just out of superdeep-freeze they weren't quite conscious enough, I'd say, to identify you on arrival.'

'What, what . . . ?'

My tongue, my throat froze. It was as if I were being sucked through the needle of a hypodermic syringe, an agony beyond all human experience and feeling.

And after a lapse of eleven Earth centuries, I was tall and grey and elderly once more.

'So this is what you and I were waiting for in the reception area!!' I managed at length to gasp.

I glanced down at Magdala. I shuddered. A claw-like hand sought to clamp itself over mine.

'Come!' she said with the same sort of cackle that had once greeted me in a clearing of an African jungle. 'We'll go find the Wilkins types, fully thawed out now, I feel sure. Let them see the outstanding results of their other experiment.'

This Side of Heaven

Time and again she stole a brief but searching glance at him as he waited for her reply. But if, indeed, he was feeling any kind of stress then neither his pale sensitive features nor his relaxed manner offered any clue.

She turned once more to the uncurtained window with its outlook of flowerbeds ablaze with June colours, trim lawns and, beyond the lawns, a belt of pine trees.

The sun rode high, the clouds were mere whispers. In the calm of that summer afternoon not one branch of the pine trees was stirring. Yet in that white-painted, overheated room she gave a momentary shiver.

'Yes, I am. — Yes, quite prepared,' she said, eyes fixed firmly on the distant pines.

The surgeon's words were cool, deliberate.

'I wonder . . . ', he said.

She swung round on him.

'Well, what is there to lose?!'

'Maybe everything you've been clinging to for the past four years!'

'What d'you mean?'

'Remember the hoping? Now it's reality — and the chance element. No stepping back

42

to the day three weeks ago. A second operation? Well . . . ' His eyebrows rose high. The way in which he slid his spectacles into their case was a gesture of finality.

'There's — there's always a chance. Must be, must be!'

The surgeon's smile was paternal.

'We all look for miracles. But miracles don't come the way of my profession all that frequently. There's nothing miraculous in what I do. I diagnose, I assess, I operate. I have my knowledge, my instruments, my drugs. Nothing supernatural.

'If all has gone to plan then your little boy will have his sight. Good sight, too, with the aid of spectacles. But if not to plan, then . . .'

'I'm absolutely sure you haven't failed,' she said quickly.

The man shrugged.

'Well, if faith can play its part . . .' He glanced at his watch. 'Go find yourself a cup of coffee. The nurse and I will be in there with your boy' — he nodded towards one of the two doors which led out of the room — 'for a quarter of an hour. Come back in twenty minutes, no sooner.'

She remained firmly in her chair, knuckles

strained white as she gripped her handbag.

'If you don't mind I'd rather stay,' she said.

'Very well. Remember, though, no emotional outburst. You cannot, of course, come in with the nurse and me.'

'I understand.'

'Always the big, unanswerable question, assuming one hundred per cent success on the surgery side. It's virtually impossible to forecast the psychological effect. The gift of suddenly being able to see everything. Maybe a little too much for him to cope with — at first. He'll need calm, comfort, patience. Every scrap of understanding you possess.' The surgeon paused and, turning towards the closed door, stared enquiringly for a moment at the white panels. 'Please do not expect any miracles.'

Within the space of ten minutes she had counted each visible branch on each of the distant pines and then checked her totals a dozen times over. She had also run and stumbled and crawled through a life-time of total blindness. And in those same ten minutes she had fretted away yet another complete life-time.

'Missus!'

'Y-yes?'

She swung round. A hospital porter filled

the doorway leading into a corridor.

'Your white car close to the railings near the main gates?'

She nodded.

'Been chasing all over the place. You'll have to shift it — quick!'

She glanced at her watch.

'Later. But why?'

'Why? It's in the way. That's why!'

'But I parked close as possible to the railings. I can't see . . . '

'**You** can't see. You're not the only one. How about all the poor devils rattling their way along them railings with their white sticks? Or would be if that car of yours wasn't blocking the way!'

'Oh, dear — I didn't realise. I was in such a state. The car park was jam-packed. Would you mind moving the car for me? I daren't leave here this minute.'

She held out the car keys.

'What d'you take me for? Enough on my plate without women like you round my neck!'

She thrust coins into the porter's hand.

'Please!'

'Okay, then.'

Depending on railings. Hand over hand. Slow. Tap, tap, tap. The unknown, danger at every step. For the rest of his life.

45

'Oh, no, no, no. Please God, please, not that!'

Her words, echoing in the empty waiting room, had scarcely died away when, smiling, brisk, the surgeon emerged from the side ward where the child was lying.

'Didn't I warn you 'no emotional outbursts'?'

'Will he have to . . . ? A failure, was it?'

'Failure? Failure indeed!' The man placed a comforting hand on her arm. 'On the contrary, the miracle you've been praying for. Your boy is fine.' The comforting hand now became a restraining hand as she attempted to make for the door of the ward. 'Not just yet. He's had minor sedation. I want him to regain full consciousness slowly, naturally. A few more minutes.'

'Couldn't I just . . . ?'

The surgeon shook his head.

'How long have you waited — four years?'

'Yes.'

'So what can a few more minutes matter?'

She did not reply.

'And now,' the man went on, 'an urgent call for me in Ward B. Promise you won't go in there until . . . ' he consulted his watch ' . . . until half past three.

'Words of warning. No repetition of that emotional outburst — and in no

46

circumstances interfere with the heavy curtains in there.'

Through the open door she watched the man hurry along the corridor, she watched as he stepped inside the lift. She waited until she heard the clatter of the lift gate then she tip-toed towards the door of her son's ward.

'Simon!' she whispered, lips pressed to the white-painted door panel, 'Simon, it's Mummy!'

She waited, breathless. Second followed second, followed second, but there was no response from the other side of the door.

'Simon, Simon!' It was no whisper this time. 'Simon!'

Still no response.

'Simon!!'

She seized the door handle then caught a glimpse of her watch. Twenty-five minutes past three. She turned slowly away and walked to the window. The sun was still high, the lawns deserted, the pine trees almost undisturbed.

'Mummy, mummy, mummy!'

From the other side of the door she heard a thud. She flung herself across the waiting room, burst through the door of the ward and slammed it behind her. Then she waited, helpless. Throughout that long afternoon she

47

had paced the white-painted waiting room or stood at its tall windows, brilliant sunlight everywhere. Now, in the deep gloom of the tiny ward with heavy ceiling-to-floor curtaining, she could see nothing.

'Simon, Simon, darling, where — where are you?'

The reply was a muffled, choking sob.

She dropped to her knees and, arms widespread, she shuffled her way over the silk-smooth parquet floor.

'Simon!!'

As her eyes at length grew accustomed to the gloom, the room began to take on shape. She found the child, now sobbing, now silent, lying face downwards on the floor.

She snatched him up and clasped the slight and quivering body to her own.

'It's mummy, Simon. Everything's all right. What — what happened? Tell mummy — please!'

'That — that thing, there. I — I couldn't, I couldn't . . . Mummy, I couldn't . . .'

'You couldn't what, my darling? Hasn't the doctor, haven't we, done everything we promised? Tell me Simon, haven't we?!'

'I fell over it. There, there. I fell right over it!'

Her embrace was savage in its intensity.

'Tell me, Simon. Is it — is it all right?'

48

'You're hurting, Mummy, you're hurting!'
'IS IT ALL RIGHT?!'
'I fell over that thing — there, there, there!'

She glanced around the dark, heavily-curtained room. There was no carpet, no rug. Apart from the couch close to the wall and a chair in one corner, the place was totally devoid of furnishings.

'I — I don't understand, love. There's nothing here you could possibly fall over. Nothing. Simon, please tell me. Can — you — see?'

'Mummy, look!'

Again she peered into the gloom.

Nothing.

Then a faint breeze stirred and briefly parted the heavy curtains.

'Look, look, again!' He thrust a hand towards the window. 'But I can't touch it. I can't touch it, Mummy!'

'Can't touch . . . ? But of course you cannot touch. That, my darling, is what we call — a SUNBEAM. And nobody this side of heaven could ever touch a sunbeam. For most of us the sight of one is really quite enough.'

Masterpiece

Hardly any other of today's sculptors managed to capture the female form in marble quite so exquisitely as Hague Parry.

Top models snarled and fought like sharp-clawed tigresses for the prestige of an hour's sitting for Parry the Great. Until the day he collapsed in the midst of photographing the flame-haired Katrina in preparation for the Vienna International Statue Award.

Within seconds Parry's speech had become slurred, the corner of his mouth sagging. He could do no more than motion — with his left hand — Katrina to leave the dais and get dressed. The right arm that directed the chisel to create miracles in marble swung useless at his side.

Old Parry was finished, they said. Never again capable of handling even a stick of chalk, never mind a superlative chisel.

Never again? They were reckoning without the Parry who had fought to the top the hard way and remained a fighter.

After months of exercises that daily drove him to tears of agony, after medical treatment that cost him his penthouse suite, his studio, the yacht, his Ferrari and his Rolls Royce, Parry began the slow and frustrating struggle back to living and sculpting once more.

At first the old skills were only dimly evident. In the beginning he was unable to afford the fees demanded by models no matter how modest. His former model, Katrina, who owed so much to Parry in her career, laughed in his face when he suggested that he pay her at the end of the year.

'What guarantee?' she said.

Parry shrugged.

'I can't guarantee anything. Only wish I could. But it's a fantastic award. I've got to try. I know I can do it. With you.'

'What award?'

'The Graffenberg. Fifty thousand pounds with heaven knows how many commissions to follow.'

'If you win, Hague Parry. Only if!'

'I can. I will.'

'And if you don't — what about my fee at the end of the year?'

'Oh, please, Katrina, look at those small pieces on the shelf over there and judge. Three weeks' work, that's all. I'm as good as ever I was. I had no photographs for them, no models. They were all sculpted entirely from memory. Don't they prove at once I'm back in form?'

Parry raised both arms and demonstrated the suppleness of his wrists and his fingers.

'Now, that miniature statue of yourself — I could almost fall in love with you as I look at it!'

Katrina turned to take a cursory glance at the array of marble figurines on a shelf. Their sculpting was skilful in the extreme, the interpretation exquisite. Her expression, momentarily hidden from Parry, registered her admiration for the work but she was careful to curl a lip as she turned to face him once more.

'Not bad,' she said. 'And to show there's no ill-feeling I'll take the one of myself as a deposit.'

Parry clasped his hands together.

'So you're agreeing to sit? And be paid at the end of the year?!'

Katrina had already picked up the miniature marble statue.

'Packing, a box, wrapping paper!' she said.

'Of course, Katrina, of course.'

'And 'of course',' she mimicked, 'a quarter of the Graffenberg award!'

Parry swallowed hard.

'That's — that's over twelve thousand! The agency told me you were now the most expensive model on their books and I was prepared — but twelve thousand . . . '

Katrina's elegant hand hovered over the door handle.

'And, of course, five hundred, in cash, for each sitting — if the sitting doesn't stretch beyond the sixty minutes.'

Parry's jaw dropped.

'Five hundred . . . ? It — it used to be fifty. But when things were going well I always gave you extra.'

'Used to be, Hague Parry. I've moved on since those days.'

'Only because I groomed you, Katrina, showed you the way!'

'Oh, face it, Hague, without me you haven't the ghost of a chance. Yes or no? Once I'm on the far side of this door you've cooked your goose. It'll be bye-bye to me and bye-bye to the Graffenberg thousands.'

Parry took a deep breath.

'You — you win, Katrina!'

'And make sure you're a winner as well,' she said, slamming the door behind her.

Within seconds the door re-opened.

'Hague!'

'Yes, Katrina?'

'This figure's rather heavy. Have it delivered to my flat, will you? Today at the latest!'

'Y-yes, Katrina. Most certainly!'

Motionless as the statue that she was to become, Katrina was poised on a high stool atop the dais in Hague Parry's studio once more. Parry had directed a spotlight to Katrina's hair, others accentuated the high and elegant cheekbones while back-lighting from three separate angles, softer, more subtle than the other lights, outlined the exquisite part-naked body. Draped over her shoulder, and contrasting sharply with her auburn hair, was a cloth of gold that cascaded to the dais.

Parry took a step forward to adjust the drape then back to the camera on its tripod.

He smiled and nodded his head.

'Fantastic, Katrina!' he breathed rather than uttered.

Katrina's perfect features were without expression.

'Worth every penny, hm?'

'Every penny, Katrina!'

From all the usual angles Parry took photographs. Then he began to seek every unusual angle.

Katrina's face hardened.

'How much longer?' she snapped.

'A few more minutes, please, I beg you. Almost there, I promise.'

Once more Parry peered into the camera's viewfinder. Perfectly still for almost sixty minutes, Katrina all of a sudden began to fidget. Irritated, Parry stepped swiftly back from the camera then just as swiftly returned to it. One hand raised as if to freeze Katrina, he pressed the shutter release and for the second time that morning he smiled.

The model's slight movement had disturbed the cascading cloth of gold. It had slipped and, for seconds until she quickly recovered it, her other shoulder and a tantalising area of naked breast had been revealed.

'You — you were magnificent, Katrina!' he said, throwing up both hands in admiration.

Katrina, gathering the cloth of gold firmly about her, rose from her stool and stepped down from the dais.

'What else did you expect?!' she said, ice in her voice.

The moment that Katrina disappeared into the changing-room, Parry crossed to the window to ponder on, for the hundredth time, the block of flawless pink-white marble standing there. In the ensuing weeks this was to become another Katrina, a passport to a renewed fame and the prize he so desperately needed to win.

With mounting excitement, Parry developed the camera film and printed the range of photographs of his model from which he would work in the weeks to come. He frowned. All but one of the pictures were mediocre. Sharpness, crispness, originality for the most part were lacking. He examined closely the photograph that was the exception.

'Fantastic!' he muttered to himself.

He hurried from the darkroom to inspect the print by daylight in the window of his studio.

Then, 'Oh, the clumsy, stupid bitch!' In the subdued lighting of the dark room Parry had been overjoyed with the photograph and its capture of that briefest of moments when the cloth of gold slipped to reveal the model's naked shoulder and breast. But in broad daylight he could now see that Katrina had moved her head a fraction at that magical moment, blurring the line of her nose and cheekbone.

The photograph, the only suitable one, was, after all, too imprecise for Parry to use as a blueprint for his Graffenberg sculpture.

'Damn!'

★ ★ ★

On the telephone Katrina was less than sympathetic. Four weeks hence was the earliest she would be available for another sitting, she told Parry.

'And the fee will be a thousand pounds!' she said.

'A — a thousand? And a whole four weeks? But that gives me less than ten days to complete the statue for the judging. There'll hardly be time for me to eat or sleep!'

'Your problem, Hague, not mine.'

For seconds Parry was silent.

Then, 'All right, all right, Katrina. I'll manage somehow. You win. Four weeks today!'

Parry replaced the receiver and put his head in his hands. Ten days to complete the statue. Ten impossibly short days!

★ ★ ★

Katrina on the dais again, motionless, the cloth of gold draped skilfully over her exquisite naked figure.

'A celebration, Katrina!'

Parry handed her a glass of wine, filled to the brim.

'To an unrivalled combination. Your beauty, my talents!' Parry drained his glass. 'Marvellous to have you back. Your glass. Empty. A fill up?!'

As Katrina was handing her wine glass to Parry she keeled over and slumped on the

57

dais. The cloth of gold slipped away from her elegant shoulder.

This time, however, she made no effort to retrieve the cascading fabric.

* * *

The statue 'Katrina' was without doubt infinitely superior to anything that Hague Parry had ever produced at any time in his career. With the rest of the entries for the Graffenberg Award it stood on the ceremonial archway that spanned the recently constructed road to the Graffenberg Museum.

Spurning all offers of help, Parry had struggled alone with ropes and pulleys and finally succeeded in raising his shrouded sculpture to the top of the archway during the night before the judging. His entry, the very last, was in position within mere minutes of the closing time for the contest.

The judges were unanimous. For the outstanding statue 'Katrina' the Graffenberg prize of £50,000 was awarded to Hague Parry.

It was hoped, the chairman of the judging panel said, that Mr Parry would now go on to grace many other suitable places in the city with examples of his inspired craftsmanship.

Twenty four hours later Hague Parry, his few remaining possessions rammed into a suitcase, was heading by a roundabout route for the airport.

There were two cancelled seats on the next direct flight to Rio. To ensure desperately-needed sleep Parry booked both.

The aircraft took off at precisely 2330 hours as scheduled. It was shortly after midnight when the police reached the departure lounge.

★ ★ ★

Without the faintest doubt, Hague Parry was a superb sculptor but as embalmer he had proved to be less than competent.

After a mere twenty-four hours on the top of the ceremonial arch near the Graffenberg Museum, Katrina, for the first time in a long and distinguished modelling career, was beginning to look distinctly downcast and droopy and grey, barely a shadow of her former exquisite self.

Two Down, Two Up

My wife's hazel eyes beamed bright as a summer's day the moment I placed the cardboard box on the table.

'Whatever can it be?' she said, ripping the box apart.

Then she saw. Those hazel eyes were suddenly as dull as a late afternoon in November.

'And what exactly d'you call this?' she said, sweeping the box off the table then stamping her foot. On mine. Hard.

'Owch. It's — er — it's a present for our wedding anniversary, our very first, darling!'

'But what exactly is it?!'

'It's a jam spoon,' I said.

'A wh-a-a-a-t? A jam spoon?!'

The words burst forth with all the sweetness of a crate of squashed lemons.

She brandished the offending article within a millimetre of my nose.

'It's — er — it's solid silver and very antique,' I said.

'It's certainly very something!'

'Please — please don't look at me like that,' I said. If there'd been enough space

60

in that tiny kitchen I'd have gone down on my knees to her. 'But it's all I could manage. I had in mind a cruet set but the best I could lay hands on was only electro-plated. I'm afraid things are a bit — well, you know — a bit dodgy at the moment. I'll do what I can, maybe, later on.'

' 'Maybe later on'. How many more times have I got to listen to that? You're like a long-playing disc. You've been saying 'maybe later on' ever since the day after we got married! And what happens? Nothing. Precisely nothing!' Again the spoon attacked the tip of my nose. 'Like this — this nothing!

'If you'd followed my advice and taken a job with Benksey six months ago, there'd've been a real present for me today. And we'd've been living in a proper house. Not just a miserable two-up-and-two-down in a tatty back street off the London Road.'

I threw up both hands.

'I'm sorry, love, dead sorry, honest. And you don't know about jobs with Benksey. I've got a feeling he's in plenty trouble. Plenty big trouble.'

My wife smirked.

'Oh, yes, I've seen one of Benksey's troubles. A fantastic big trouble. I walk past it all the times I can't afford the bus fare

61

from town. That big trouble's a mansion!'

'A mansion? You sure?' I said.

'Calling me a liar?!'

'No, no, darling!'

'Come on. I'll show you Benksey's very nasty load of trouble. Where's the car?'

I shrugged.

'In the back street.'

'Well, what are we waiting for?'

'The car.'

'The car? It's out there, you said, waiting for us.'

I tried to take her hand. She thrust mine aside.

'I'm sorry, love, but no licence, no test certificate, no insurance, four bald tyres and a petrol tank full of nowt but fresh air!'

Her tone was icy, bitter.

'I seem to remember Benksey running a few Rolls Royces. One for himself, one for his wife and at least a couple of spares for his kids. Okay, I'll pay the bus fares.'

★ ★ ★

Benksey's house had an enormous garage, a swimming pool, rose gardens, orchard, a sprawl of conservatories, a range of stables, a vast paddock and what I took to be a helicopter pad.

62

We trudged up a wide sweep of drive and climbed the steps to a broad terrace. It was deserted. My wife tugged on the ornate bell handle. A peal of bells echoed and re-echoed through that enormous Benksey establishment.

We waited and waited. Nobody came.

She gave another tug, savage this time. Still nobody came.

'I don't think Benksey can be at home,' I said.

My wife gave me a withering glance.

'Could it be their Bermuda weekend? Or the Seychelles maybe?'

I stepped to one side for a peep through a mullioned window.

'Look,' I said. 'Just look! Funny sort of weekend, taking all the furniture and carpets with them.'

The floors were bare boards, there wasn't one item of furniture in sight, not a single picture on the walls. We walked the terrace from one end to the other. Every room looked as though a removal firm had gone in and done its job with total efficiency.

We walked down the steps of the terrace, then all the way around the Benksey mansion. Every downstairs room was as empty as the first one.

'Better check on the Rolls Royces!' I said.

The garage, big enough to accommodate a tennis court, was empty.

In silence we retraced our steps along the drive to the main road, then called at the tradesmen's entrance of an adjacent residence.

A woman in an apron answered the door. She glowered at us.

'No odd jobs, no double glazing, no drains for cleaning, no clothes pegs. No matter what you're flogging — it's no, thanks!' she snapped.

'We're looking for the Benkseys,' my wife said.

'You're not the only ones. I'm sick and tired of hearing the name.'

'The house looks empty,' I said.

'Well, it would be, wouldn't it, if nobody lived there any more.'

'Nobody lived . . . ?'

'They've gone.'

'Gone where?' my wife said.

'The Continent.'

'What part?'

'Haven't a clue. Mr Benksey inherited a lot of money, they say. He went to collect.'

'When?'

'December could be.'

'What about Mrs Benksey?' my wife said.

The woman shrugged.

'Some tale about not going with him. I reckon he's ditched her for some fancy bit on the Continent.'

'So where's Mrs Benksey now?'

'A two-up-and-two-down crummy dump somewhere off the London Road.'

My wife swallowed hard.

'Bit of a come-down, hm?'

'What do you think?!'

I took my wife's arm and we turned to go. I could have been wrong but I felt as though she was holding on to me a bit tighter than usual.

Back in our two-up-and-two-down in that street off the London Road, I slumped into an easy chair, kicked off my shoes and, hands behind my head, I lolled back.

'Maybe we'll bump into Mrs B. one day,' my wife said.

'Maybe.'

'Now, come on, you knew a thing or two but you weren't letting on. Out with it. What happened to Benksey and when?'

'You heard what the woman said. She was right. It was December. To be exact, old Benksey scarpered on the thirtieth. The Croydon bank hold-up ten o'clock that morning. By three o'clock in the afternoon, I reckon he'd be safely clutching the loot in a taxi driving him down the Champs Elysées in gay Paree. A one-handed job. I never imagined he'd cope on his own,' I said.

'And how about Mrs Benksey?'

'The waiting game for her. Until it's safe to join him. Maybe,' I said.

'How long, d'you reckon?'

I shook my head.

'Ask old Benksey. Who can tell? Forsaking a mansion love-nest for a two-up-and-two-down suggests all kind of things.'

'You mean there's another woman . . . ?'

'Not very far out of Paris . . .'

My wife gave me a luscious first-anniversary kiss.

'Okay, you win, love. Let old Benksey carry on with his sort of game.'

'So you can see now what might've happened to me, to us, if . . .' I said.

'I can, my darling. I can see all right.'

'Oh, I was forgetting,' I said, 'Another little anniversary gift!'

I pressed a purse into my wife's eager hand.

'Whose?'

'Guess!'

I winked.

'That woman in the apron?'

'Well, she wasn't giving much away so I . . .'

'Cunning, lovie! So we carry on as usual and bubbles to the Benksey types?'

'Right, my darling! There's nowt to touch a steady little line of shoplifting. With a crafty handbag-snatch here and there.'

The Selling Side

Reckon I ought to have felt a whole trunk load of gratitude for Cromarty. Yet, when little Mac and me passed him on our way through the carousel doors of the Grand Majestic, all I felt was a faint twinge of sorrow, nothing more, for the guy.

'Keep the change!' I called over my shoulder to Cromarty in my best uptown voice.

He dived and scrabbled for the coins as they bounced and rolled along the sidewalk. For good measure I slung him the butt of my half-smoked Havana.

Mac's features remained gritty hard. He didn't give Cromarty so much as a backward glance.

Ten years, it must have been, since Cromarty cut across my path. Ten years and ten million dollars away. Did he recognise Mac and me? I'm never likely to know the answer to that one.

I'd jumped out of the Old Country on account of a deadly existence as a pen-pusher. Canada had the lot, they said. But I couldn't unearth it.

And it was pen-pushing all over again, this time for a guy in Montreal, until little Mac dragged me free. Within a month of gripping a Canadian pen, I was wielding an axe. The kind of axe you swing first then it takes over and swings you. I was a lumberjack.

That job just about killed me. Lumberjacking handed out all the punishment I could take aboard. And more. There wasn't the slightest need to pitch big Cromarty at me as well.

But there was never any shortage of dough in the lumberjacking game. You could stash away a fortune. Rough going though. Even the regular come-again-next-spring lumberjacks had never been pushed so hard, seven days, every week. By nightfall I could only just manage to flop into my bunk. Not like Cromarty, though. Big restless Cromarty.

That man-mountain would stump the length of the log cabin swearing he could find some better way with lumber than just axing it. He reckoned he knew exactly where the easy dough was to be found.

'On the selling side of the racket, you dopes!' Cromarty roared. 'The selling side!'

'He's dead right, fellers,' Mac said. 'Selling it — not felling it. But you gotta have the business experience, remember, Crom!'

69

There was a roar from odd-man-out Cromarty.

'Experience? Experience?! Them city guys in their fancy tuxedos? Reckon I could . . . '

Then the camp boss poked his head round the door and Cromarty's mouth clamped shut.

And it was ten years on when I really got to know what Cromarty reckoned he could do in competition with the city gents.

'Everything okay, fellers?' the boss shouted.

And even Cromarty had to grunt 'Yeah!' with the rest of us. Deep now into the lumber-felling season you daren't try cutting across the boss-man. By that time in the fall, jobs weren't exactly hanging from every other Douglas fir in the forest.

★ ★ ★

It was a crisp, bright backwoods morning the time the boss teamed me up with Cromarty. Both of us stripped to the waist, swinging those axes good as pendulums. I was getting somewhere fast, working with man-mountain Cromarty, all his magnificent brute strength perfectly directed and controlled on the other side of the tree. Cromarty was as graceful with that axe as some old-time society dame with her fancy fan.

And just as if he could read my thoughts and resented my grudging admiration, he would send chips of fresh sharp wood flying into my face. Those chips hurt a lot, he knew, but never for a split second did he let up. He used to swing and cut as if he detested the very guts of every tree in that vast forest.

Teaming up with Cromarty, though, offered a whole heap of compensations. The more lumber you felled the bigger the pay-off. And Cromarty could put down far more trees than any other lumberjack in the north.

So, when you played it double with Cromarty and the chips were flying like monstrous mosquitoes, you forced yourself to think about the way you were stacking the extra cubic feet in lumber credit and you struggled to dream about all the dough you were stashing away in your bank account.

Mind you, Cromarty didn't get it all his own way all the time. Maybe some lumberjack would stop swinging, lean back on his axe and gasp, 'A let-up, Crom. A few minutes let-up, what d'ya say?'

And Cromarty's reply was always a hand to his buddy-lumberjack's throat. One hand, not two. Just one of that guy's hands was big enough and powerful enough to throttle a man.

'Pick — up — that — axe. We lost fifty cube already!'

We'd been swinging steady for an hour when, for a change, it was Cromarty who stopped. He'd stopped to laugh at me. My body glistened with sweat, my back feeling it was broken in a dozen places, my face and shoulders blood-raw from the flying chips.

'Take it easy, Crom!' I gasped, struggling to straighten up.

Cromarty wiped the sweat from his little piggy eyes and you could've heard his roar back on the sidewalks of Montreal.

'You miserable little slug!!'

On the other side of the clearing Mac must have spotted the way things were going. Mac, who'd dragged me away from that city desk and dumped my pen down the first sewer pipe we came across.

'Hiya, Cromarty. Come on over. What d'ya make of this?!' Mac shouted.

Cromarty relaxed. If somebody was looking for advice there was no guy in camp quite like Cromarty for thrusting it down your throat.

He flicked his axe. The blade buried deep in the bole of a Douglas fir. He strode towards the spot where Mac was standing.

The brilliant sun, shining straight into the

face of that king of the lumberjacks, must have momentarily blinded him as he picked his way between the tree stumps. No guy anywhere in sight loved Cromarty enough to yell a warning 'Timber!!' And Cromarty couldn't have heard the death groan of a Douglas fir about to drop.

As Cromarty reached the centre of the clearing, the trunk of the fir, thick as a railroad car, that Mac and his buddy had been working on, gave the brute-lumberjack no chance to sidestep.

All of a sudden I was wanting to be back at the desk in Montreal, casting an eye over the stenographers and wishing I'd enough dough to take the taller blonde out on the town. Wishing that the only rough stuff in my life was the slap across the face I landed when I tried to kiss her in the corridor.

There was a long silence. All the other lumberjacks had stopped to lean on their axes and watch. Like me and Mac they were hoping.

Any other guy but Cromarty would have made a big imprint in the earth and stayed there until it was decided to dig him out for the funeral. But not big bull Cromarty.

Within seconds the end bits of the branches of that fir tree began to flicker ever so soft-like. Then whole branches began to stir. They rustled, then slowly they began to part. Cromarty's head appeared. With a jerk and a thrust of massive shoulders he freed himself from his temporary grave.

He straightened up, and, in slow motion, wiped his mouth with the back of his hand then brushed away the dirt from his face, his arms and his legs. Those little piggy eyes began to search around the clearing. It wasn't long before they settled on Mac.

Cromarty let out a deep, deep belly-laugh and with a dozen giant strides he was onto the little guy.

We all watched, helpless. Poor Mac. Never in all my life had I seen a man die but not quite.

For gentle, good-hearted Mac the lumber season, with many to come, was as good as over.

Cromarty didn't do himself a whole heap of good though. His bank account lost a thousand cubic feet because there was no more work done in the clearing that day. Boss or no boss we all beat it back to camp, taking it in turns to carry little Mac. We slid him into his bunk where he lay, twisting, groaning and moaning all the way through till morning.

Hours later, Cromarty followed us and,

without a word, dived straight into his own bunk.

Except for the gut-wrenching noises from Mac you could have sliced the silence with Cromarty's super-weight axe.

★ ★ ★

For the rest of that lumber season big Cromarty was forced to go it alone.

The Cromarty-Mac episode seemed to kick the heart out of the rest of the lumberjacks. Nobody was sorry when, the night after the first fall of snow, the boss looked in again, this time to say, 'Pay-off tomorrow, you guys. Tomorrow, first light!'

For the first time in weeks we heard Cromarty's voice.

'I'll take mine now!'

'I said 'tomorrow, first light'!' the boss said.

The boss, bending his head backwards to speak to Cromarty towering above him, was on the losing side this time.

The little eyes got lost under the bushy eyebrows.

'Give!'

The boss dragged a wad of bills from his inside pocket and quickly counted out Cromarty's pay-off.

The last bill had barely touched the table top when Cromarty, thrusting the boss roughly aside, scooped up his dough and rammed it into a duffel bag. Then, striding across to his bunk, he grabbed the rest of his gear and stowed it on top of his pay-off.

There was such a sensation of relief among the lumberjacks that this roughest and toughest of seasons had at last come to an end that — well, they mightn't have forgiven Cromarty exactly for beating up little Mac, but they might've said, 'Be seeing you in the spring.'

But the callous glance that Cromarty flung in the direction of little Mac's bunk set the pattern on things. They turned their backs on him. Big Cromarty, for always, was going to be frozen out of lumberjacking.

And maybe he was able to read all the other guys' thoughts because, as he slung his kit over his shoulder and opened the cabin door, he bellowed, 'Sellin' it next time, suckers. Sellin' — not fellin'. Just like little Mac said. So watch for it!'

Yep, Cromarty was finished with lumbering. But he wasn't the only guy looking for a change of job. Mac was forced to. And I just wanted to.

Came that night then, about ten years on, I reckon. Mac and me smoking fat cigars on our way into the bright lights and sweet music of the Grand Majestic, to our own special table, head waiter licking the carpet in front of us. Maybe hitting the high spots could cost us a few thousand dollars a throw. So what? Dough was coming in ten times the rate we were able to spread it around.

And Cromarty there, on the outside without so much as a look-in.

Sure, big Cromarty had achieved his ambition okay. Like Mac and like me he'd got right on to the selling side of the lumber racket.

But it was only little stuff that scrawny hobo Cromarty was handling.

I never yet came across a guy who got real rich and fat scrabbling for loose change or flogging boxes of matches outside the Grand Majestic.

Powder Trail

The style of his mohair jacket was beyond reproach, the fit as precise as if he had been poured into the garment.

He made a further, even more admiring, appraisal of his reflection in the mirror: hair immaculate, the knot of the silk necktie demanding no more than a millimetre adjustment.

She threw aside the evening paper and glanced up.

Her tone was caustic.

'Satisfied with what you see?'

He took another even more searching look.

His bland response in no way disguised his pride.

'It'll do!'

'You've read the latest, I suppose?' she said.

'Skimmed the headlines,' he said, his attention almost wholly directed to the necktie.

'Saw the report about another break-in? Just along the avenue this time.' She looked at the clock. 'And, as usual, between nine and eleven. The fifth so far this month, the paper says.'

He raised his chin and took a step towards the mirror for an even closer inspection of the silken knot.

'That guy — if it's the same one all the time — makes it look dead simple. Seems he's got just the knack,' he said.

'You'd think the police could do something,' she said.

He was smiling. The knot in his tie was now perfect.

'Oh, they will, they will. Cunning mob. They'll be holding back, I reckon. One false step and he'll be straight behind bars. That is, of course, if he acts thick!'

'What d'you mean, 'acts thick'?'

His smile changed to a laugh as he glanced briefly in her direction.

'If, say, he happens to leave his Mini on double yellow lines then dives off to do a quick little job! Police? Catch him? Sure they will. They're wizards when it comes to crime on double yellow lines.'

'Oh, why can't you be serious? Why don't you spend an evening at home once in a while?'

'How would that help?'

'Well, at least you could tackle an intruder!'

'Tackle . . . ? Tck, tck, tck! You know

how I detest violence!'

'In case your posh suit and tie come in for a battering?!'

'Now, who's not being serious?!'

'Frankly, I just fail to understand. Are you totally, utterly devoid of feelings? Can't you understand how nerve-twanging it gets, here on my own, night after night, with all these break-ins?!'

He laughed again, this time totally without mirth.

'What? Frightened of getting stolen yourself?'

'Here we go again. Serious talk and you shy off right away. Of course, it's not about getting stolen myself.'

She crossed to the window and, drawing back one of the curtains a grudging inch, she then paused.

'Put the light out!' she said.

His tone was scathing.

'What ever for?!'

She stood, gripping the edge of the curtain.

'Quick, quick!'

With exaggerated reluctance he flicked the light switch.

'Don't tell me. I know. He's there, just beyond the street lamp on the corner waiting till I've gone out.'

'See for yourself!' she said. 'Please — please don't go just yet!'

He joined her at the window and, with a gesture of irritation, dragged back both curtains for a fuller view of the avenue.

'Yes, I can see!' he said. 'And I recognise him!'

'Recognise . . . ?'

'Hangs around most evenings. He's waiting till Bill Longstaff, Harry Fynne and I leave for our session at the club. He's the fancy man Bill's wife entertains while Bill's knocking back the pints. Or it could be Harry's good lady!'

She glowered at him.

'Silly, dangerous, saying things like that. Does Bill know, does Harry know?'

'I never ask questions. Maybe, maybe not — but it never stops them going out.'

He drew the curtains back in place.

She was persistent.

'What makes you think it's Mrs Longstaff or Mrs Fynne?'

He winked.

'I can't be one hundred per cent sure. He could be waiting for somebody else. You, for example!'

'Will you please, for once, talk some sense!' she said, as she crossed the room to put on the light. 'Make a joke of it if you like — I can't.'

'It's that necklace — apart from yourself — isn't it?!' he said. 'What do I keep on telling you? Get rid. What was the last offer?'

'Eleven hundred and fifty.'

'Should've grabbed it with both hands. Your great, great grandmama won't be caring all that much now about her jewellery! Think of the load of worry you could be saving yourself.'

'I never had any real intention of parting. And never will have. Never!'

The hands of the clock pointed to nine. He took a further admiring glance at himself in the mirror.

'It's about time I went . . . '

' 'For my couple of pints and a session at the dartboard',' she mimicked.

'But if I happen to come across your nine-to-eleven man I'll give you a ring,' he went on.

She shrugged.

'For that thought straight from the heart — thank you. But don't bother to come tearing home after ringing. You'd be less than useless.'

She followed him along the hall. He paused as he stepped into the avenue.

'Look!' he said softly, 'He's still there. Nip over, shall I, and tell him I won't be back till after eleven? See you. S'long!'

For fully a minute she kept an eye on the

man. He made no move. Before slamming the door she took a further look. She turned both keys and hurried back into the living room.

Her hand went at once to the telephone. The police were for ever telling people, 'If you see something suspicious report it at once. Better be safe than sorry'.

She dialled 999. The operator's response was immediate.

'Which emergency service?'

Er — suppose — suppose her husband happened to be right?! Suppose the man in the avenue wasn't the nine-to-eleven man. Suppose he was really waiting until Bill Longstaff or Harry Fynne was out of the way for a secret assignation with one wife or other.

The suspect, frantic to clear himself, could easily blurt out more than was good for anybody. The police knew exactly how to get people talking.

'Which emergency service — please?!'

'S-sorry,' she said at last, 'I'm sorry. A mistake. A wrong number!'

She made her way up the stairs. The necklace, with other items, was in her jewel case. Mm. Far too obvious a place. Better hidden somewhere on its own. Somewhere absolutely unexpected.

Fine. But where?

The obvious, of course. Don't hide, wear it! Keep it round her neck all night. No burglar would ever dream of searching that far. No burglar would . . . She drew a sharp breath. Well, these days he just might!

She shuddered.

And yet, and yet it seemed the only way.

She drew the necklace over her head and, holding the clasp at the nape of her neck with one hand, she pressed the pendant to her throat with the other. She looked long and admiringly at the effect in the dressing-table mirror. Apart from the family-heirloom aspect, how ever could she have thought of selling such an exquisite piece? She attempted to fasten the clasp. It came apart. The necklace slid to the dressing table top then snaked to the floor.

'Damn!'

The problem all over again.

Where, where could she hide the precious article?!

She went into the bathroom. Pressed into the soap perhaps? No, no, the soap was too hard. Behind the hot-water tank? No again. Tried it, years ago, hiding a pair of earrings. Still there. They weren't costly but the sentimental value was high. Not high enough, though, to warrant paying what the plumber had demanded for temporary removal of the tank.

She retraced her steps to the bedroom. She paced up and down, the damaged necklace clenched in her right hand. Here and there she paused to consider the safety offered by a corner cupboard or inside the hat band of her husband's homburg used only for funerals. Or under the edge of the bedside rug, held in place, perhaps by a few stitches. Or, perhaps, beneath the mattress. Or inside the light-fitting over the dressing table. Or the fitting at the bed-head.

Every option picked up, examined then discarded.

Nothing, nowhere seemed to offer complete safety.

But, surely, there must be somewhere!

Where, though, where, where?!!

Got it!

The talcum powder on the dressing table! Yes, yes! Bury the necklace deep in powder!

No burglar would ever dream of looking in there. And if he did he'd have a frightful job getting rid of the powder trail. A sitting duck for the police.

She went to bed at half past eleven. The evening had been uneventful. Before undressing she dug her fingers into the talcum powder. The necklace was safe.

It was long after midnight, much later than usual, when her husband crept into the bedroom.

'Where've you been?' she said.

'With the lads, of course,' he said.

'Till this time?!'

'Yes. Did he come?'

'Who?'

'Your nine-to-eleven man!'

'No!'

* * *

They awoke late next morning. After a hurried breakfast he left for the office. She was still in bed. As she lay there she began to wonder idly where her husband had spent the time after his club closed for the night. And whether the burglar had been on the prowl again.

Oh, the necklace? Safe?!

A glance in the direction of the dressing table at once gave reassurance. The container of talcum powder was still there.

She tumbled out of bed. A ray of sunshine crept into the room. The top of the dressing table seemed dusty. She ran a finger over the wood. Dust certainly, but not ordinary dust.

Quickly she tipped out the talcum powder. A perfumed cloud obscured everything but the fact that the precious necklace had gone.

The burglar's sixth victim this month. Why, oh, why hadn't she sold as her husband suggested?!

All his fault really. It was his clear duty to stay home. Callous, insensitive beast! She flung herself across the unmade bed and she burst into tears.

Then, without interest, without enthusiasm, she began to tidy the room. Her husband's new mohair jacket had been thrown carelessly over a chair along with trousers, shirt, the silk tie. She picked up the jacket to drape it on a hanger. There were traces of powder on the lapels.

Oh, no, not him! It couldn't be him! Couldn't be?

Yet he did go out most nights around nine and he was rarely home until after eleven.

Her fingers flicked at the traces of talcum powder adhering to the fabric. She sniffed. A faint unfamiliar perfume assailed her nostrils.

She sniffed again. And again.

Ugh, muck! What absolute muck! She wouldn't be found dead using cheap, shoddy, talcum powder like that awful rubbish!

Earl-y in the Morning

For a man who had never quite escaped from land or sea, master mariner James Clancy had always been a pretty high flier. Until the day his wings were clipped by a marriage to a raven-haired lass from Dublin. Scarcely had the bridal bouquet begun to wilt than that girl was laying down the law like some high-court judge. No more dodging up and down the China coast, no more idling across the broad Pacific. Captain James Clancy was granted grudging permission for short, regular trips to the continent and back, once a week. One pipe of tobacco per day was permitted provided that it was consumed on the back porch or, if the weather happened to be inclement, in the potting shed. And there were carpet slippers in the hearth at The Anchorage every Saturday and Sunday evening.

But, somehow, James had managed to get away with the pair of pigeons.

'Never come across a seaman before with a taste for pigeons — except in a pie, cap'n,' I said to Clancy in the saloon of his ship one bright Monday morning.

'You customs wallahs! All the same. Years behind the times,' Clancy said. 'Haven't you heard yet? Parrots went out about the time of Long John Silver and old Captain Hook.'

'Because they opened their beaks too much, cap'n?' I said.

Clancy pointed to a trio of wooden monkeys huddled together on a shelf.

'A very nasty mind you've got, Mr Customs Man. Hear no evil, speak no evil, see no evil.'

I completed formalities and stepped on deck.

Clancy's pair of pigeons were cooped up in a basket which swung from the ship's rail. Poking and pecking at each other, they didn't seem in the least happy with their strange surroundings. Sleek, handsome creatures they were. Clancy must have paid a great deal of money for them, I thought. But that was Clancy. At least that used to be Clancy. Before the wedding day. Ever since I had known him he had been a man of fad and fancy, pursuing a new hobby with a zeal approaching fanaticism during a spell of shore leave, then promptly dumping it overboard for something else that, at the time, seemed infinitely more attractive. Last year he was shivering with excitement at raising mink, months earlier it was mushroom-growing in the cellar. Once it had been model railways, then came a brief flirtation with philately. And now, clearly it was pigeon-fancying.

I poked an idle finger through the wickerwork of the basket. Those pigeons had a distinct taste for the flesh of customs officers. So, not without reason, I took an instant dislike to the birds. And in my own mind, I nurtured an idea that the raven-haired Mrs Clancy was nothing of a pigeon-fancier either.

Her interests were more likely to lie in the more exclusive dress salons of Dublin, in lipsticks and necklaces and sumptuous rugs than any of her husband's fleeting hobbies.

So, Cap'n James Clancy, I said to myself as I sucked a tender forefinger, there must have been a rare old tussle in that love-nest of yours on the outskirts of Dublin. And your dainty little spouse managed to come out firmly on top. You will have received extremely precise instructions to remove your obnoxious feathery pets from that smart villa and take them off to sea with you. Ah, ah, Cap'n Jim, although you may be master of your own ship on the high seas, back at The Anchorage you're nothing more than a junior officer, only the second mate, in fact.

I'd stepped from the gangplank to the

quayside when I suddenly remembered the book of raffle-tickets which our garden fete committee had thrust into my unwilling hands. Clancy was always the man for a harmless flutter. I went back aboard.

'All entirely unofficial this time, cap'n,' I said. 'Not anxious to be lumbered with complaints about you missing the chance of winning a bottle of rum or a rich fruit cake in the garden party swindle. I'll gladly nurse your winnings until you drop anchor again next Saturday.'

Clancy's smile was indulgent.

'How much?'

'As little as you like, provided it's not less than a couple of fivers.'

Clancy dragged some notes from his wallet.

'Thank you, Cap'n James. Any particular preference for numbers? Lucky ones?'

'Make sure there's a two in them some-where,' Clancy said.

I handed over the raffle tickets, wished Clancy happy sailing and a safe, prompt return.

'No need to try smuggling any rum next weekend,' I said as I left the saloon, 'With all those chances I wouldn't be surprised if you scooped the pool.'

In their basket Clancy's pigeons were still

swinging on the ship's rail. Calmer now, poking their beaks through the wickerwork, at last they seemed to have found their sea-legs. They showed no further interest in my finger even when I gingerly inspected the identification rings on their ankles. I scratched each poll, briefly just in case, to show that we were now the best of friends.

The next Saturday, Clancy's ship came splashing back into home port twelve hours earlier than expected, in ample time for the garden party. I should have realised, of course, that Clancy would get his navigation instructions from the dark-haired first mate at The Anchorage. Come hell or high water — I don't suppose for one moment that she'd put it in such a tangy way as that but her dainty phrasing would be equally effective — come hell or high water. Clancy must make the first tide on Saturday. Not only the first tide but he had to get himself smartly ashore so that together they would cut a dash at the party. Captain James would be decked up in his number-one uniform, ablaze with gold braid and brass buttons, while Mrs Clancy was to be turned out in all the up-to-the-minute finery that her favourite Dublin salon could muster.

I picked up the Clancy ship in my binoculars when she was a good three miles away from the harbour. It was such a superb morning that if she had been as much as ten miles off-shore I would have spotted her readily from the look-out. The seagulls, frantic about something, were fighting and wheeling and screeching overhead when, just as the bows of Clancy's ship cut the waters between lighthouse and fish pier, I glimpsed a pair of gulls, close together, circling the vessel, topmast high.

The pair had probably been snatching all the generous pickings from the galley and that would be the reason for the ill-tempered circus of other gulls overhead. The lucky pair had been gorging themselves on the remnants from Clancy's breakfast table.

Although I'm no bird expert, I did notice something strange about that pair of gulls which arrived with Clancy's ship. They were not wafting their wings in the lazy, powerful style of seagulls. It was a swifter, more jerky action. I kept the binoculars trained on the birds. All at once they ceased their wheeling and, dipping like air force fighters suddenly latching on to their prey, they made a swift bee-line for the shore.

The two birds were not, of course, seagulls. They were Clancy's pigeons and, doubtless, they carried a message of undying love and obedience clipped to their legs. They were a pigeon post, advance notice to Mrs Captain Clancy that her husband was docking on the early morning tide in accordance with instructions. And customs officers and stevedores willing, he would be stepping across the threshold of The Anchorage no later than mid-day.

Highly novel, rather astute, Cap'n Clancy, I thought. What a clever jimmy you are. Or could it be that Mrs Clancy was the brains of the outfit? Perhaps the pigeon post idea was hers and Clancy's latest hobby had thus received an unqualified domestic blessing.

Roof-top high, the pigeons soared on their homeward flight. In that glorious morning sunshine there was a crisp glisten on their feathers. Even their claws appeared to sparkle.

I was delighted that Clancy had made port twelve hours ahead of schedule. The garden party was not exactly depending on his presence but, without his generously-open wallet, the proceeds could well be twenty five, even thirty, punts short of estimates.

I left the customs watch-house and hurried along the quay. They were looping the first hawser over a bollard as I reached the ship. Clancy was on the bridge.

'Slacken off there, aft. Now hold her

forrard, hard as you like. Hold her, hold her!'

Anxious that my business with him and his ship should not delay Clancy one single moment more than necessary, I straddled the gunwale and slid on deck long before anybody had given thought to lowering a gang-plank.

'Welcome home, cap'n!' I called to the bridge.

Clancy gave me a wave and a minute later we were shaking hands.

'Don't you ever sleep, Mr Customs Man?'

'Never on lovely mornings like this. Back much sooner than expected?' I said.

Clancy tapped the side of his nose and he winked.

'Got my docking instructions before ever setting sail on Monday.'

'From the mate?' I said.

Clancy solemnly nodded.

'Right!'

'So plenty of time to fling your money about at the fete this afternoon.'

'If wallahs like yourself don't tie me up in your red tape half the morning.'

'Come snow-white clean and I promise express treatment,' I said. 'How are the pigeons? Enjoyed their continental trip?'

Clancy nodded.

95

'Where are they then?' I said.

'Gone, gone!' There was mock sorrow in the voice. 'The moment they spotted land they jumped ship.'

'After breakfast though!'

'Of course!'

'Greedy, graceless wretches. Not to worry though, cap'n,' I said, patting Clancy's arm, 'I think I saw them heading fast and furious for The Anchorage. Ought to be there by now. Looked the real homing type, the pair of them.'

I followed Clancy to the saloon and, within half an hour, we had completed all customs requirements.

'See you at the garden party swindle, then,' I said.

Something crunched beneath the sole of my shoe as I stepped on the open deck. I knelt to retrieve it. A pigeon's identification ring.

'I notice they got undressed before they departed, cap'n!' I called.

Clancy appeared at the door of the saloon.

'What a brilliant bunch of sleuths you custom wallahs really are. Never miss a trick!'

I felt my chest swell beneath my tunic.

'Thank you!'

'Know anything about pigeons, Mr Customs?'

96

'Not a thing.'

'Well, for a start, they detest being decked up!'

I can't recall a more successful garden party. Sunshine, dry under foot, plenty of variety, crowds spending up to and beyond the hilt. Clancy was there, as expected, resplendent in gold braid and brass buttons but, in spite of his impeccable turn-out, he was as dim as a Toc H lamp compared with that sparkling dark-haired wife of his.

'Goodness me, just take a peep at those diamond rings the woman's flaunting. Did you ever ... ?' my wife hissed as we stood together, manning the tea-and-cream-cake stall.

'Jealous?!' I hissed in reply.

The kick on my shin under cover of the table cloth converted my hiss to a gasp.

I had, in fact, already taken a long and close look at the rings. The sparkle from the diamonds in the afternoon sun was something that only a blind man could possibly miss.

And my mind went back to a similar sparkle. Still in sunlight but much earlier in the day. Overhead at about roof-top height.

But is there anything a customs officer can really do when he's busy with a tea-and-cream-cake stall at a busy garden party in the middle of a summer's afternoon? Apart from hacking off a couple of bejewelled fingers with a cake knife?

And you never could be sure of what precisely you saw, with the sun in your eyes, so earl-y in the morning.

The Memories Man

In pursuit of an imaginary speck of dust,
Whiteman flicked a cotton cloth over the
counter of the coffee bar. The pattern of the
cloth suddenly seized his eye: the blue and
the white stripes. He screwed the fabric into
a ball and rammed it hard on the counter.

He'd get rid of them all. Those cloths had
been a job lot. Shoddy and cheap, they had
been bought at the time when every penny
was important.

The hands of the clock pointed to half-past
eleven.

Whiteman leaned over the counter to
peer beyond the glass doors. In rain which
had been torrential throughout the evening
the promenade remained deserted. Most
potential customers had already scurried past
on their way home from seafront cinemas and
amusement arcades, more concerned about
catching last buses than dawdling for ten
minutes in his coffee bar. In the past half-hour
not a single person had crossed the threshold.

Whiteman could close with confidence.
The trifling profit to be derived from the odd
cup of coffee would be more than swallowed

up by the cost of the electric lights which flooded every corner of the premises.

Again the coffee bar proprietor glanced towards the wet promenade, shiny in the red and gold of his neon sign, the sign announcing that his premises remained open until midnight, seven days a week. He surveyed the luxuriantly appointed bar, the image of himself in the bronze-tinted mirror on the far wall. He was tall and lean, immaculate in white Cossack-style overall: a man of seventy who might readily pass for fifty-five.

Whiteman treated himself to a congratulatory nod of the head and a confident pursing of the lips.

Business-wise, Whiteman had arrived. But not without superhuman effort. An utter stranger, he had known year upon year of a bitter, often ignominious, struggle to establish himself in this seaside town. Cragwick welcomed outsiders — but merely as holidaymakers with money to spend. Only the coldest of shoulders was offered to those who moved into the town and attempted competition with local establishments.

Whiteman retrieved the ball of blue-and-white cloth and once more thumped the counter with it.

The coffee bar was to remain open, as

100

advertised, until midnight.

He turned to throw the light switches serving most of the empty alcoves and failed to notice the woman. She had slid, swiftly, quietly, into a seat at a table close by the counter.

The hands of the clock were now at eleven-forty.

The customer dragged off a rain-hood to reveal a tumble of hair, white as newly-fallen snow. The eyes were the eyes of an old woman, yet her slim and shapely figure, the elegance of her legs, the stylish shoes and modish raincoat suggested to Whiteman a much younger person.

He eyed her appraisingly.

'Mm!' he murmured. 'Mm, mm!'

He bowed.

' 'Evening, madam. May I serve you coffee?'

'Thank you. Black!'

'Certainly, madam!'

The woman's eyes traced the activity of Whiteman's hands as he filled a coffee cup. Then they switched to the sight of the screwed up blue-and-white cloth.

If, at that moment, Whiteman's ears had been conscious of any sound but the whirring of the coffee machine they might have detected a faint gasp from the lips of his elegant late-night customer.

He served the coffee. She acknowledged it casually and dribbled coins on to the table. As Whiteman picked up the money she seemed preoccupied with his hands. Those carefully tended members were a source of pride to Whiteman. They revealed nothing of the thousand and one menial tasks he had been driven to perform in the years of bitter struggle since the end of the war: refuse collecting, sweeping the floors of amusement arcades, scavenging the beaches for holidaymakers' litter.

Back once more to his stance behind the counter, Whiteman turned to flick with a duster then re-arrange the stocks on the glass shelves. Blue-wrapped bars of chocolate and packets of white-cartoned biscuits he handled one by one then, with military precision, set them back in place. Blue wrappers precisely alternated with white cartons. Whiteman frowned momentarily and at once varied the display.

He glanced at the clock. Ten minutes to midnight. Not only was the woman continuing her obsession with his hands but seemed absorbed in his movements as well. Her interest produced a faint smile from Whiteman as from time to time their eyes met, either directly or through the mirrors that lined the walls. But from the woman there was no evident response. She sat, tight-lipped, face devoid of expression, coffee untouched.

'That cup must be cold, madam. Let me bring you another one.'

The woman at once leapt to her feet. Her chair went careering across the smooth tiled floor. And, with one final glance at Whiteman's hand resting on the blue-and-white cloth, she hurled herself through the glass doors then vanished into the darkness beyond the range of the lights of the coffee bar.

Midnight barely five minutes away. Whiteman glanced at the still swinging doors. He shrugged and picked up the neglected coffee cup.

The atmosphere in the bar was warm, oppressive. He worked slim fingers around the high collar of his Cossack-style overall. His neck showed crimson where the stiffness and tightness of the fabric had chafed the pale skin.

It was at this moment that a second late-night customer appeared. Head down, the brim of a trilby dragged low over his features, the man burst through the doors of the coffee bar as if every hound of hell was in pursuit.

'Coffee. Black. Plenty of sugar!'

Head still lowered, the man dived for a table in one of the alcoves.

Whiteman, glancing swiftly at the clock, and frowning, filled a cup and hurried with it to the customer. As he crossed the tiled floor the man's eyes avidly followed Whiteman's feet.

'Seventy-five pence, sir!'

Whiteman thrust out a hand. The man fumbled through his pockets, flung generous coins on the table then slowly raised his head.

The proprietor of the coffee-bar gasped. He was confronted by a caricature of a face that thrust forward to within inches of his own. It seemed as if the jaw had been broken then set in a fashion utterly foreign and useless to its purpose, leaving the mouth lop-sided. The lips, agape, revealed a foreshortened tongue and gums entirely devoid of teeth. Whiteman swung swiftly away to seek the comforting isolation behind the bar counter.

The customer's face bore an expression that might have been interpreted as a sickly smile. With care he put the cup to his mouth and, flinging back his head, sluiced the contents down his gullet. Then he bounced up and his departure from the coffee bar was as swift as his arrival.

Midnight.

Whiteman threw the switch that controlled the lights outside the coffee bar. He hastened to fasten the main doors. One arm raised to thrust the upper bolt into position, he was hurled back by his third late-night customer, a mountain of a man, hatless, in streaming-wet coat. The stranger, towering over Whiteman, urgently scanned the coffee bar proprietor's upturned face.

For chilling seconds, rain and wind tore unhindered through the wide-open doors. Whiteman, in an attempt to close them, sidestepped the man.

As if he were no more than an empty cigarette packet, the stranger pitched him aside and kicked both doors firmly shut.

Whiteman seized the edge of the counter.

'I'm — I'm sorry, sir. We're closed!'

The man gave an easy laugh.

'The doors are closed. You are still open. Coffee, a quick cup. That's all — for the moment!'

Whiteman's grip on the counter edge tightened.

'I said, 'We're closed', sir!'

'And I said, 'Coffee'!'

Whiteman swallowed hard. He glanced towards the clock. Four minutes past midnight. The stranger, seated now at a table, was staring hard at him. Twice Whiteman let an empty cup slip from his fingers. Twice he filled a cup to overflowing. And all the time the man continued to stare.

'You're taking your time with that coffee!'

'Sorry, sir. Coming!'

On its way to the customer some of the coffee slopped into the saucer.

'I beg your pardon, sir. I'll bring another.'

'Another?' The customer was now smiling. 'Another?! Oh, forget it. You seem extremely nervous. Any reason?'

'Er — no. — No!'

'You imagine I'm here to rob you. Yes? I've been watching. One eye on me, the other on the cash till. Oh, it's not your money I want. Look, plenty!'

The stranger thrust a hand inside his dripping raincoat and drew out a wallet. He waved a twenty-pound note at Whiteman, then placed it on the table.

'For one cup of coffee. Keep the change. Don't look so astonished. After travelling all this way it's worth a great deal more than twenty pounds simply to sit and rest for a while. You made a fuss over spilling the coffee. Spilling a trifling fluid like coffee. Strange, very strange.'

Whiteman's fingers sought the chafing collar of his overall.

'I've — I've had an extremely long day. I'm tired.'

'Even-stevens. You've had a very long day, I've had a very long journey. Please, five minutes.'

Striving to display a nonchalance he patently did not feel, Whiteman leaned over the table to pick up the twenty-pound note. At once the man's eyes riveted on Whiteman's neck.

Quickly Whiteman made for the far side of the counter.

'T-travelled a fair distance, have you, sir?'

The stranger's smile was disarming.

'At a rough guess — one hundred thousand kilometres.'

'One hundred thousand . . . ?!'

'Give or take the odd thousand. — And worth every single millimetre now that the end's probably in sight!'

Rainwater, dripping from the stranger's coat, had created a pool on the cafe floor.

'You — you should've taken your coat off, sir,' Whiteman said, concerned more likely for his floor than his customer. 'Not at all pleasant for you sitting like that.'

The man flung back his head and guffawed.

'Not at all pleasant?! Rain and snow, frost and sleet, winds piercing as a surgeon's scalpel. None of these trouble me any more — after standing in them half a lifetime.'

Once more Whiteman ran fretful fingers around the edge of his Cossack-style collar. He snatched a glance at the cash till, then the telephone alongside it.

The hands of the clock were pointing to a quarter past midnight.

He drew a deep breath.

'Is — er — is that so, sir? It's now long past my usual closing time. I must ask you to leave!'

The stranger eyed him above the rim of the coffee cup.

'I shall be staying until you are ready to go. Then we leave together.'

'What d'you mean?!'

'Precisely that. We'll be leaving your coffee bar together.'

Whiteman lunged for the telephone. A cup and saucer shattered on the floor. A table and chair skidded crazily over the polished tiles to crash into other tables and chairs.

A grip like a vice settled on Whiteman's outstretched arm.

'Don't waste your time — or mine!' the customer said and slowly, relentlessly, he twisted the arm until nerveless fingers let the telephone crash to the floor.

Suddenly the grip on Whiteman's arm

relaxed. Off balance, he lurched forward. Once more the hand descended. This time to wrench away the high white collar.

Wholly visible now was a broad scar, puce-coloured, slashing the whiteness of the surrounding skin. It stretched from ear to the point of the shoulder.

Pursing his lips, the stranger gave a nod of satisfaction.

'My brother,' he said, 'well remembered your feet. He had good reason to remember. He used to be such a handsome young boy — used to be. And my niece could never, never forget those hands of yours.

'Yet — yet we couldn't be absolutely certain. After forty-odd years, one solitary faded snapshot could never be the final piece of the jig-saw, Mr — er — er — Whiteman. So now the scar. We'd never forgotten the sight of it. Your pride and joy. Won not in the heat of battle though. Just while playing soldiers before the war. — Remember that war and a camp, forty-five years ago — and one hundred thousand kilometres back? Memories now flooding, Mr Whiteman?'

The lips of the stranger began to tremble, the eyes filled with tears. Almost with reluctance, his gaze shifted from the scar on Whiteman's neck to the window.

Outside, pressed to the wet glass was the

face of the woman with the old, old eyes. Beside that face was the face with the twisty jaw. Whiteman's third late-night customer beckoned. The man followed the woman into the coffee bar. She made at once for the counter to seize the blue-and-white cloth.

'Remember?' she said, thrusting the cloth into Whiteman's terror-stricken face.

The man with the jaw edged between Whiteman and the woman. His clumsy mouth battled with the words.

'Of course he remembers. How could he possible forget the filthy blue-and-white uniforms, tens of thousands of them?'

Whiteman's eyes darted from one to another.

The tall stranger who earlier had removed his dripping raincoat was now putting it on. Then, stepping behind the counter, with a single contemptuous sweep he cleared the shelves of their blue-and-white display.

The smile was grim as he seized Whiteman by the neck, fingers biting deep into the scar.

'And for the rest of his life — such as it's likely to be — he will go on remembering. It is our job to make him remember. Every second of every minute of every day of that eternity in hell. Remember, Mr Whiteman? Remember Auschwitz — AUSCHWITZ? — S.S. Oberleutnant Weissman?!'

The Little Tin God

Parkinson had limped into that sleazy Colombo bar more because of an urge to escape from himself than to consume warm beer. As he eased himself on to a high stool there was a tap on his shoulder.

'Kildale! Never expected seeing you in a dump like this!'

'The prices suit my pocket!'

Parkinson snatched a glance at Kildale's jacket. In spite of its obvious age, the cut and the quality still lingered: a good deal more than might have been said for his own shabby khaki drill outfit.

'Thought you'd be making the usual pile from the tea-plantation,' Parkinson said.

Kildale grimaced.

'Pile of debts, you mean.'

'Dodging creditors down Colombo's back alleys?!'

'No, no. Looking for help!' Kildale's eye quickly assessed Parkinson's skinny forearms, the cadaverous features, the shabby khaki. 'Or maybe handing some out.'

'And that's where I come in?'

'Not exactly. Hardly expected seeing you

this side of Suez. Thought you'd skipped it back home to Britain.'

Parkinson shrugged.

'Starvation's more comfortable in sunshine!'

'I could save you starving — for a spell. I'm looking for somebody to keep an eye on the plantation while I'm in dock. Three, four weeks at the most. Interested?'

'Could be.'

Parkinson gulped warm beer and grimaced. Kildale laughed.

'I'd lay on something better than that pig-swill. And nothing much to do. Just a watching brief.'

For years and years Parkinson had been hearing the whispers. 'The war kicked the guts out of poor old Parky.' 'Useless devil!'. 'Never known him not fall down on a job.' Well, perhaps this time . . .

'Sounds fine!' he said.

'Wait for it, Parky! All your keep, plenty of tea, no shortage of booze.' Kildale gave a wry smile. 'But no pay. I couldn't afford a salary.'

Parkinson shrugged.

'What's that thing about beggars and choosers?!'

Kildale gave Parkinson's shoulder a comforting pat and handed him some notes.

'Great. This'll get you there. Sorry it isn't more. I go into hospital on the twentieth, so aim to arrive thereabouts.'

'Thanks. I'll be there. Thanks very much!'

As Kildale left, Parkinson drained his glass and glanced at the others in the bar. He could guess how their minds were working. 'Parky at it again', 'The soft touch as usual', 'Fancy poverty-stricken Kildale falling for it', 'Same old sob story.'

The breeze from a lazy overhead fan stirred the note which Parkinson had slid along the counter.

'Drinks on me, all round!' he said and, jerking himself from the stool, he limped into the withering heat of a Colombo back alley.

★ ★ ★

It was mid-afternoon as Parkinson climbed the verandah steps of Kildale's bungalow, his only welcome the buzz from a swarm of insects beneath the overhanging roof. Puffing and panting at Parkinson's heels, the taxi driver flung a suitcase to the floor and thrust out both hands, palms uppermost.

'Pay, pay!'

Parkinson slapped coins into the outstretched hands. The man scuttled back to his brake. The vehicle swung round

113

and Parkinson's eyes followed it until it disappeared along the narrow winding track to the valley below.

The dust lay thick in Parkinson's throat. His voice was faint, its tone diffident.

'Anybody at home?'

Apart from the buzz of insects there was silence.

'Hullo there. Anybody at home?!'

The ferrule of his stick thumped the wooden floor of the verandah.

The Sinhalese houseboy who emerged from a curtained doorway was taller than Parkinson and, even when the latter drew himself up to full height, the mouth of the Sinhalese was on a level with the brim of his hat.

Brown eyes scrutinised the battered and bursting suitcase, the shapeless khaki drill, the cracked shoes and, finally, Parkinson's diffident expression.

' 'Afternoon. My name's Parkinson. Presumably Mr Kildale told you I was coming.'

Again the Sinhalese glanced at the suitcase and the shabby shoes.

Yes, he had been warned somebody would be arriving to stay while Mr Kildale was in hospital. Parkinson had a distinct feeling that he ought to apologise for the intrusion, for his clothes, for the suitcase, for his highly inconvenient time of arrival. Damn! How

114

was it, he wondered as he searched the immobile features of the houseboy, that almost anybody could make him feel so puny, make him frantic to curl up inside himself? Even this arrogant, dusky imitation of a nineteenth-century butler! Could he never again bring himself to rapping out orders in case they were ignored? Better have a shot, though, for Kildale's sake.

Parkinson turned and slumped into a wickerwork chair.

His back now to the Sinhalese, he said, 'I'd like some tea!'

There was a swish of curtains then silence.

Parkinson waited.

When at last it was served the tea was good. Parkinson drank appreciatively. The houseboy waited behind the chair beyond the range of vision.

'What's your name?'

'Kala!'

'Damn fine tea, Kala. More, please!'

Fearfully, Parkinson waited for a refusal that failed to materialise. The Sinhalese snatched the tray and hurried indoors.

The insects continued to buzz. Parkinson stretched wide his arms then tilted the brim of his hat against the glare of the afternoon sun. No wonder, he mused as he glanced sleepily at his shirt and slacks, that the houseboy had eyed him with such disdain. Even at the outset of the journey to Kildale's plantation the clothes had been far from clean. They were filthy now after the crazy drive along the track through the foothills. Dust and sweat streaked his hands and arms, the dust lay thick on his face. He grimaced as he licked his coated lips.

Making scarcely a sound, the houseboy placed a fresh tray of tea on the verandah table.

'Thanks!' Parkinson drained a cup with a single gulp. 'Mm. Nice!'

There was no reaction from the Sinhalese.

Parkinson thrust back the brim of his hat and swung round.

'Can you lay on a bath?'

The face of the houseboy was devoid of expression. His eyes roamed over the grimy arms, the dusty clothes.

'No bath here!'

'No bath?!'

'No.'

'Oh, come off it, boy!'

'I fill a barrel with hot water.'

'A what?!'

'A barrel.'

Parkinson searched the dark face. A leg-pull? No bath? Not true, of course. Certainly Kildale was having a struggle

116

to make ends meet but somewhere in the bungalow there must be a basic necessity such as a bath. Ah, he'd got the idea. This Sinhalese houseboy didn't think he was a fit person to use Kildale's bathroom. Why, the black-faced . . . ! Easy, easy, easy, now. Three whole weeks to go. Better not start off on the wrong foot. The boy had produced tea without any fuss so, maybe, a little later on . . . And, after all, what difference did it make? Hot water was hot water no matter how it was dished up.

'Do just that. Fill a barrel, steaming hot!'

Once more Parkinson lolled back in the verandah chair.

Three weeks of stop-gap, three solid weeks of merely looking-on with an assurance of regular meals and a sound roof over his head.

Maybe this brief interlude would set him on his feet again, restore some of the confidence that the ending of the war had snatched away.

Parkinson's fingers flicked at an insect as it settled on his cheek and his stick, which he had propped against the chair, clattered to the verandah floor. Bending to retrieve it, he glimpsed a cobra gliding swiftly across the floor boards. He shot up, stick aloft. The Sinhalese appeared.

'No, no, no!'

The stick landed with a thud that shook the flimsy verandah.

The body of the snake writhed and twitched as the metal ferrule explored the battered head.

'Never, never kill cobra. Never. Now SHE come.' The quivering forefinger of the Sinhalese stabbed in the direction of Parkinson's chair. 'And SHE kill. Why, why you do it? Why you come to our plantation?!'

Parkinson guffawed.

'SHE will come? Who the hell's SHE? What are you babbling about, boy?'

'The cobra's mate. And when she come she kill!'

'Ah, well, we can die only once, Kala. And I've been living on borrowed time for years and years. But you can leave the cobra's wife to me.' Parkinson twirled the stick between his fingers. 'Don't forget that bath-barrel in all the fuss. With plenty of soap.'

Smiling, Parkinson sank back once more in the chair and lit a cigarette. Chin resting on chest, he idly watched the flies investigate the cobra's lifeless body. He stretched and yawned. If that Sinhalese didn't get a move-on with the barrel of water pretty soon he'd be far too sleepy to clamber into it.

118

'The bath is . . . Look, look, look! She come. I told you, I told you!'

Before Parkinson had time to raise his stick, the fangs of the female cobra had buried deep into the leg of his slacks. Then the creature glided swiftly over the verandah's edge to disappear into the bushes beyond.

There was a smug look on the face of the Sinhalese.

'White man, I told you! No doctor here. You die. You die very quick!'

Firmly grasping his stick, Parkinson hurled himself out of the chair.

'Okay, boy, I'm going to die. So I'll let you into a secret. If I'm going to snuff it then I'm going out spotlessly clean. Show me the way to the bath-barrel!'

And, as if conducting a ghost, the Sinhalese houseboy led Parkinson through the curtained doorway then disappeared.

As he peeled off his grimy clothes, Parkinson could hear shouting in the distance. The shout surged to a roar. The bungalow was quickly surrounded by a screaming mob of men and women.

The mob began to chant, 'White man kill cobra, cobra's wife kill white man. White man kill cobra, cobra's wife kill white man!'

Parkinson burst out laughing. He laughed so heartily that he found it difficult to clamber up the side of the tall barrel and slip into the steaming water.

Dying, was he? Was he now?! On the contrary, he hadn't felt better for years. Not since the war, in fact. Curious, having to kill a mere cobra simply to give his morale a boost. Damn curious. Watch his step and, for the next three weeks, he could be a little tin god with this lot.

Leisurely soaping himself, he joined in the chant with the mob outside now struggling to catch a glimpse through the window of the crazy white man who took a bath in preparation for death.

'I don't feel the least bit dead — yet!' he bellowed at them.

And, rubbing the soap away from one eye, he flung a knowing wink at his artificial leg which stood in a corner of the bath-barrel room.

The Birthday

Stepping gingerly over the railway track she lifted the teddy bear from his corner of the window sill. After dusting and dusting yet again the already gleaming white paintwork, she put the teddy back to his endless watch of the street below.

At the station the train was waiting. The guard held a silent whistle to his lips. There seemed to be no urgency. The passengers in carefully arranged groups along the platform made no move to step aboard.

As if performing some act of devotion, she knelt to uncouple the locomotive and polish its already gleaming livery. Then she uncoupled, dusted and recoupled the dustless coaches. With a final glance at the bed, its smooth pillow and creaseless coverlet, she closed the door and went down the stairs.

On a table in the sitting room there was a photograph of a young boy, beside it a silver, perpetual calendar. With a motion akin to reverence she turned the calendar to Tuesday, 15 July.

There was a knock at the door. The milkman.

'Just three pounds seventy-five this week, love!'

She handed over coins without so much as a glance at him or at the small change he thrust into her open palm. She was watching, over the man's shoulder, a solitary child on the far side of the street. The milkman followed her gaze.

'A naughty lad!' he said, winking.

'Naughty?'

'It's only the fifteenth.'

'Yes, yes, I know,' she said and a frown momentarily seized her forehead. 'But why 'naughty'?'

'He ought to be in school. They don't break up till Friday.'

The man pocketed the money.

'See you next week.'

'Thank you,' she said, her eyes still glued to the sight of the truant boy who, down on one knee, was shooting a glass marble again and again at a discarded cigarette packet.

'Sonny!'

The boy's head jerked up. She was on the shaded side of the street. He did not at first see her.

'Sonny!!'

She beckoned. Reluctantly the boy picked up his marble and crossed over to her door.

'Yeh? What?'

She eyed him up and down. Untidy hair, hands filthy from encounters with the gutter, grey pavement dust on both knees.

'No school today?'

His manner was at once bellicose, defensive.

'No. What's it got to do with you?'

'Nothing really. Except it's funny seeing a boy your age playing in the street this time of day.'

'Well, I've been.'

'Been? Been where?!'

'School, of course.'

'And landed yourself in trouble?'

He nodded.

'If you like.'

'How old are you?'

He fidgeted.

'Ten. Why?'

'Fancy some orange squash?'

'Not arf!'

'Wait there.'

She disappeared indoors to return with a bottle and a beaker.

The boy seized both. Feverishly he opened the bottle.

'Careful. Not all over my nice clean doorstep — if you wouldn't mind!'

He drank noisily, pleasurably, gulping down a beakerful at a time.

Then he belched, equally noisily, and,

clearly, with a great deal of satisfaction.

She winced.

'You've got a lot to learn, sonny!'

'What d'you mean?'

'Oh, it doesn't matter. Tell me, why aren't you at school?'

He shrugged.

'Kicked out,' he said.

'Why?'

'No good, I s'pose.'

She took the now-empty bottle and beaker.

'What's your worst thing at school?'

' 'Rithmetic. That's why I got kicked out this morning.'

'Kicked . . . ?'

'Teacher said, 'Get out of my sight!'.'

'Well, it's about time you went back — or went home!'

'And get a bashing from our Mam? What d'ye take me for?!'

'But you can't stay out all day. What'll your Mum say when you do get home later on?'

The boy winked.

'If I get home about four she won't twig, will she?!'

'Mm, I see. You like playing marbles?'

He rolled the solitary marble in his palm. 'Smash!'

'Would you like more?'

'Would I?!'

'Wait there.'

He was back on the sunny side of the street when she returned.

'Here you are!'

He ran to her. She thrust a tin into his outstretched hands. He strove to lift the lid. It opened unexpectedly. Marbles, scores of them, bounced and scattered in all directions: down the pavement, across the road, into the porch, into the hallway.

He dived along the pavement in pursuit.

'Wicked! Fantastic!'

When at last he had rescued every marble outside, he elbowed his way past her to continue the rescue operation in porch and hallway. She flinched as the toes of his shoes scuffed polished linoleum and skirting board.

At length he got to his feet.

'Sure you've picked up every one?' she said.

'Oh, yeh, yeh!'

'And what else should you say?'

A smile spread across the grimy features.

'Okay, missus. Ta, — ta a lot!'

'And now it's time to get yourself cleaned up.'

'Cl-cleaned up? Whaffor?'

'Your Mum won't want a dirty-faced little

125

boy going home for dinner.'

'My Mam? I never go home for dinners. You get 'em at school.'

'Then clean yourself up ready for school.'

'Told you, didn't I? They kicked me out!'

'So you get no dinner?'

He shrugged.

'But I can play.' He rattled the box of marbles. 'I can play 'til tea-time.'

'Fancy some dinner with me?'

He snatched a glance through the open door at sunshine on the other side of the street.

'Cold meat and chips then apple pie,' she went on, 'and maybe more squash.'

He glanced once more at the sunshine then at the smiling woman.

'And no cleaning up?'

'Well, not much!'

'And not now?'

'In a couple of hours.'

Clutching the tin of marbles he escaped into the sunshine.

'I'll be back!'

She had long finished her meal when he returned. Tin of marbles tucked under his arm he burst into the kitchen, whistling some wholly tuneless tune. He established himself on the chair at the table and set the tin close to his elbow.

'How about that dinner?'

'How about . . . ?!'

'You said I had to come back.'

She stood, hands on hips.

'Too late. None left.'

'None left?' He searched behind the sternness for a smile. In vain. 'But you told me!'

'To be back in a couple of hours.'

'Well, I . . . '

'I know, you forgot. Well, you're not the only one who can forget.'

He slid slowly from the chair and picked up the marble tin.

As his hand reached for the door knob she rumpled the tousled hair.

'But maybe I could find a little bit — when you've washed those filthy hands!'

Brow deep-furrowed, again he placed the marbles on the table. At the sink he thrust fingertips gingerly into a bowl of water then at once looked around in search of a towel.

'A wash, not a splash!' she said, holding out a cake of soap. 'Nothing to eat until they're absolutely spotless. Not a crumb!'

He grabbed the soap and washed. Quickly, resentfully and again most ineffectively.

She shrugged, turned her head away for a secret smile then filled a plate with meat and chips. The promised apple pie with custard followed.

When he had finished the meal she pointed to the remains of custard round his mouth.

'Now, wash your face!'

'What d'you take me for, a cat?!'

She seized him by the hair. He wriggled, he bellowed, he cursed. She washed his face, his hands and the grimy knees.

'You — you're crying!' she said, laughing. 'A big boy like you, crying!'

'I'm not, I'm not. It's — it's your soap in my eyes!'

With infinite gentleness she dabbed each eye with a corner of a towel then she dried his face, hands and knees.

Grasping both his shoulders she stepped back.

'Now I can see what you really look like.'

'You're worse than our Mam!'

'And you are just a baby, crying like that.'

He struggled to escape from her grasp.

'I'm not, I'm not!'

'All right. Soap in your eyes then. Now, some more orange?'

'I wouldn't mind,' he said gruffly.

'Say 'please'.'

'Aw, come on, missus. You — you know nowt about kids.'

'D-don't I?!'

He seized the beaker of orange squash and nodded briefly at her in acknowledgement before putting it to his lips.

'Me crying, you said. Me? There's tears in your eyes, missus, not mine!'

Turning swiftly away to face the sink, she said, 'Would — would you like a real treat?'

'Yeh!'

'Come along,' she said, wiping her hands carefully on her apron.

He followed her up the stairs.

The teddy bear, the model railway and the bed were just as she had left them earlier in the day.

His knees thumped the floor. Grasping the locomotive with both hands he turned it over for inspection.

'Not electric!' he said with scorn.

'No, no. Clockwork. Electric's dangerous!'

'Dangerous? Oh, get with it, missus. You're old-fashioned. And so's your bloody old train set. Seen 'em in the shops, haven't you? They're all electric! Any case kids don't want trains no more. It's all electronics. Computer games and that.'

He glanced up to find himself alone in the silent bedroom.

Leaving the locomotive athwart its track,

coaches on their sides and uncoupled, passengers scattered in all directions, the guard lying prostrate between the lines, he galloped downstairs. She was in the sitting room, studying the photograph. Alongside was an iced cake with nine candles.

'Somebody's birthday?'

She nodded.

'Yours?'

'No, no!'

'Thought it couldn't be. Only them few candles. His, is it?' He jerked his head in the direction of the photograph. 'Let's have a look.'

The moment that his fingers touched the frame she slapped his face.

'D-don't you dare!!'

He let out a gasp and, hand pressed hard to his cheek, he fled from the room.

'Oh, oh. C-come back. I'm — I'm sorry. I'm so sorry!' she called.

By the time she reached the front door he was running helter-skelter down the street.

She gave the locomotive a more vigorous polish than usual before setting it back on the rails. She coupled up the coaches. She rescued the guard. She was re-placing the passengers in their original tidy groups when there was a light tap on her shoulder.

The words were soft.

130

'The marbles? Can I have 'em?' he said.

'They'll be there where you left them,' she replied without looking up.

With added zeal she returned to the passengers. He remained standing beside her.

'Go on with you,' she said, her head still down. 'Go on, get them!'

Down below there was the rattle of marbles in a tin box.

'Missus!'

She wiped her eyes with the corner of her apron.

'Missus!!'

She scrambled to her feet.

'Yes?'

'I'm off!'

She reached the head of the stairs in time to catch a glimpse of him, tin of marbles firmly clutched under his arm.

'Don't — don't go yet!'

She tore down the stairs. He was waiting. Suspicion, resentment, impatience fought for expression.

'The train! Is it — is it really so old-fashioned?' she said.

He studied the tearful eyes.

Suspicion, resentment, impatience slowly evaporated.

'Er — well — er — mebbe, mebbe not.

Mebbe last year it'd be — er — quite all right!'

The kiss was wet. It was clumsy and most inexpertly directed. And totally unexpected. It landed on the point of her chin. And then he was away, down the street, scampering like a terrified rabbit.

Net Prophet

Sick and tired of the fishing game, I was desperate to escape from Cragwick. And I was growing more and more frantic to meet the sort of woman I could happily wed and settle down with. But, in our tiny seaside village, there wasn't one wench I could really take a shine to. And seeing so many attractive women on my rare trips to London and other places didn't help. I remembered best of all a wench in Blackpool. She was on display outside a promenade sideshow. In big illuminated letters it said 'Queen of the Sea'. She was wearing a golden crown and a long white robe. She sat motionless, her green, green eyes looking far out across the ocean. I just stood and stared. Jimmy Hardcastle had to dig me hard in the ribs.

'You've got some hope, landing a wench like that. So come on. Come on, quick!'

The coach back to Cragwick was due to leave in twenty minutes. I shrugged. We left.

★ ★ ★

133

My mother used to spend most of her time propped up in her four-poster in the front room of our house in Cragwick's Mariner Row.

On the rare occasions she did get out of bed and move around the house she wrapped herself, waist to toe, in a blanket and she walked, leaning heavily, on a pair of sticks. Her greatest pleasure seemed to be the bathroom. Father had had one built specially for her next to the kitchen.

Whole days she'd spend in the bathroom, splashing and singing. Maybe I've given the idea that Mother was a pale, drawn-looking elderly woman. Far from it. That mother of mine was youthful and lovely, serene as the North Sea on some golden June morning. Blue-green eyes, copper-coloured hair down to her waist, skin smooth as pearls.

She was for ever begging me to find a wife and settle down in Cragwick.

'I really can't believe you haven't come across some nice girl in the village. There's a lot of your father in you. For years and years, so they tell me, he was on the look-out for somebody different. Then he found me!'

An utterly devoted couple, Mother and Father. Absolutely, totally wrapped up in one another. How ever they managed to spare the time to bring me up — I was an

134

only child — I'll never know.

Life for me as a youngster had been wonderful. Except at school. Nothing wrong with the lessons, just school dinners. Most of the time the food nearly choked me. Day after day the teachers used to snap and snarl. Never bothered to chew my meat properly, they said. So when it was beef or pork or lamb or even sausages I slithered my share on to somebody else's plate. Altogether different, though, the days we had cod, haddock, plaice or skate. I'd gobble up my own helping and any others going spare. Like Mother and Father I loved fish.

After schooldays I drifted into the inshore fishing game, first repairing the wooden fish boxes and mending nets then baiting up the hooks and the crab and lobster pots.

In a year or two, I was off to sea in a fishing coble, one of the very few ways of making a living in Cragwick.

Mother died when I was twenty seven. How my father managed to survive the parting I'll never know. I suggested moving inland right away. But, like me, Father demanded his fish fresh every morning from the jetty. And, now that he scarcely ever stepped out of doors, he would have gone crazy staring at bricks and mortar instead of the ever-changing face of the North Sea.

So far as I remember Father never had a job. Yet there was always plenty of money in the house. From time to time men from London, Leeds, Birmingham and Glasgow called to buy old coins and jewellery that father kept in a padlocked oak chest under the fourposter.

About six months after Mother passed away, Father said, 'Have you still not come across a Cragwick wench you fancied, son?'

'Fancied — but not enough,' I said.

'Take a tip from me. Get yourself into the big time. You and Jimmy Hardcastle've been messing around in twenty-foot cobles far too long.'

'Big time? Fine! But tell me how. Trawlers cost thousands and thousands!'

'Oh, I could buy you a little trawler, son. Hardcastle's got his skipper's ticket. Then you'd be into seine netting and drift nets. Try your luck farther afield. Somewhere off the coast of Denmark, say. Make a fortune and, who knows, net a wealthy bride into the bargain.'

I laughed.

'How d'you imagine a trawler and bigger catches could find me the sort of woman I've got a fancy for?'

'Well, I came across your mother. It's high time we had a woman about the place again.'

Early next morning Father called me into his bedroom. The table beside the four-poster was piled high with bundles of bank notes.

'This lot should buy you a trawler and kit you out as well.' Father pointed to the oak chest. 'Plenty more where that came from if you happen to run short.'

The trawler we bought, Ocean Princess, was sea-hungry and sleek as a greyhound. And wayward as any woman. In spite of all the latest gear — echo-sounder, direction finder, radar and all that — she always seemed set on thrusting us miles beyond where Jimmy Hardcastle and I planned to shoot the nets.

It was a night awash with moonlight. We hove to, a league off the coast of Denmark — we had planned three leagues, by the way, but the Princess was having none of that — only Jimmy and I on deck, the others in their bunks below.

We trawled deep, we trawled long. Next to nothing.

'They're all up top, maybe, attracted by the moonlight,' Jimmy said.

We put out the seine nets. Almost at once a vast struggling, tumbling, silvery harvest.

Jimmy was all for getting everybody on deck.

'We'll never cope with this lot!' he said.

'We'll cope all right,' I replied, then suddenly wondered why I'd said such a thing.

But we coped. As the last few cran of fish slithered into the Princess's holds, I glimpsed a human form, naked, amid the struggling fish.

'Jimmy, you all right?!'

I glanced up quickly. Jim was still manning the winch, still fully clothed.

'Yeh. What's up?'

'Could've sworn you'd toppled in with the catch, starkers!'

Then I saw. A woman. Among a myriad struggling fish she was slithering, floundering, utterly helpless.

'Jim, quick!'

Together we leapt into the hold atop the catch and, between us, hoisted the woman to the deck.

'A — a flippin' mermaid!' Jim said, open-mouthed as a dead cod.

'Quick,' I said, 'get her covered up!'

We carried the wriggling, dripping creature to the deckhouse where Hardcastle flung his duffel coat over her naked shoulders.

There was now time to take a proper look at our catch.

I gasped.

Compared with this fish-woman from the

coast of Denmark, that green-eyed queen I'd gaped at on the golden mile at Blackpool was a scrawny old crone. Except for the occasional flip of her long and elegant tail, she sat motionless as a lovely pink marble statue.

Slowly the duffel coat began to slide from her shoulders.

'She — she must be feeling frozen,' I said, gingerly sliding the coat again over her shapely form.

The frown on the exquisite features was little more than fleeting as she thrust aside the covering.

Jimmy smiled.

'After the North Sea maybe she's feeling sweltered in here. Wonder if she's peckish as well?'

He thrust out a small haddock. The finely-etched eyebrows rose in disdain.

'Too little, you think?' I said.

'Too dead more like. She's used to eating 'em all-alive-oh. So now what? Back into the briny with her?'

'Not likely. I'm taking her home!'

'Home? Don't be so daft!'

'I don't mean home to Mariner Row,' I said. 'Fix her up in the baiting shed. The big filleting tank. Oceans of water, plenty of fresh fish.'

There was a sudden glint in the green-blue eyes. She reminded me of my mother except that she was younger and far more beautiful.

I swallowed hard. I was wishing Hardcastle would suddenly find some reason for going on deck or below and staying there. He didn't.

* * *

We nosed quietly into Cragwick harbour as dawn began to streak the night sky. We tied up at the fish quay and sent the crew home right away.

The quay was deserted. Jimmy Hardcastle and I carried our precious slippery catch to the baiting shed. She winced as we gently lowered her into the filleting tank.

'What's up, d'you imagine?' I said.

'Fresh water. She prefers the salt. Trouble, trouble, trouble, I'm telling you. Come on, breakfast. Decide what to do with it — her — later!'

I snatched a glance at long auburn hair, at coral lips no more than a whisper apart as if they were about to say something.

'I'm staying,' I said quietly.

'You must be bonkers!'

'I'm not leaving till tonight. Then she's

coming home with me.'

'But your father!'

I shrugged.

'Think, man, think!' Hardcastle continued. 'She's never likely to settle on dry land.'

Our captive was now sitting on a stool at the desk where we made up our accounts.

'Settled enough at the moment anyhow!' I said.

Inspecting the contents of the desk drawer, she had come across a piece of broken mirror. Something sounding suspiciously like 'Ooh!' escaped from the coral lips.

'A net full of nowt but trouble, I'm telling you,' Hardcastle said.

'Come back tonight after dark and give me a hand, Jim.'

★ ★ ★

From dawn until long after dusk I sat alone with my mermaid in the baiting shed. Dead though they were, she ate quite happily the codling Jim had brought before leaving for breakfast. When I shuddered at her offer of a share in the raw fish she gave me a most bewitching, understanding smile.

Throughout that day we exchanged not a single word. Yet, in some strange fashion, we were able to talk by thoughts alone. There wasn't the slightest doubt about her wanting to stay ashore. And I was determined she was going to stay. I had fallen hopelessly in love with this exquisite creature from the depths of the North Sea.

Although it was late evening, my father, hair and beard carefully trimmed, neat collar and tie, was on the doorstep when Jimmy and I arrived with my mermaid. Jim swore he'd not uttered a word to the old man beforehand.

From the moment we sat the fish-girl in my mother's rocking-chair, my father's eyes never once left her. He kept on nodding his head, she kept on tossing hers. They seemed to be exchanging confidences in the way that, earlier in the day, she and I had talked without making a single sound.

At bedtime my father indicated to her the front room with its four-poster.

'Oh, no, you don't!' I was about to say but Father must have anticipated my reaction for he quickly said, 'I'll be using the spare room upstairs.'

When my mermaid was safely tucked away in the four-poster, Father whispered, 'Where is it, then?'

'Where's what?'

'The dowry!'

'Dowry? What're you talking about?'

'All the way across the North Sea and no dowry?!'

'Dowries suggest weddings, father.'

'Exactly, son. Why d'you imagine I bought that trawler? Why a trip to the coast of Denmark? For quality, riches.' Father jerked a thumb in the direction of the front room. 'The quality's there all right, but the riches . . . ' He paused to frown. 'Maybe she wasn't planning to get herself netted. Or maybe you shot your nets a fraction too soon.'

'Would you mind? I haven't a clue what you're on about!'

Suddenly my father seemed a long way off. I snapped my fingers.

'Now, when I got your mother,' he said at last, in a strange faraway voice, 'she had a thick rope round her dowry.'

'Got — my — mother?!'

'Caught her, netted her. Did it never dawn on you that your mother was a mermaid?'

'Oh, no!!'

'But oh, yes. What d'you imagine we've been living on all these years? An extremely handsome mermaid dowry. And there's enough left to buy more trawlers and to keep us in comfort for the rest of our days.'

'I don't — I don't understand.'

'The dowry your mermaid mother brought out of the sea. In the oak chest. The custom. Mermaids with a fancy for married life on dry land always bring a dowry. Riches easy come by, of course. Ships carrying vast fortunes have been getting sunk ever since the year dot! See, son?'

Next afternoon Jimmy Hardcastle and I headed the bows of Ocean Princess in the direction of the Danish coast once more.

I didn't tell Jim I wasn't greatly interested in bulging fish-holds but I made it clear I was all for quick turn-round. I was frantic to get back to my green-eyed mermaid. She'd be outrageously pampered, I knew for certain, by my father in the house on Mariner Row.

Forty-eight hours later, holds bursting with fish but no more mermaids and not a sign of any oak treasure chests, we were alongside Cragwick's fish quay.

Before the deckhand had a chance to secure the mooring ropes I was tearing up Mariner Steps three at a time.

At our house in Mariner Row all was silent.

'Father!'

Nothing.

'Father!!'

I dived blindly into the front room and

stumbled over the oak chest. Pinned to the counterpane of the empty four-poster was a note.

'Took just enough from the chest to buy me a deep-sea trawler, son. You're welcome to the rest. She says the dowry, in two big chests, slid away just as you netted her. She can pin-point the exact spot. What a lovely lass. Never dreamt I'd strike it lucky twice. Go on, have another shot. But, please, not off the coast of Denmark this time — there's a good lad.'

Gone All Native

It was a Saturday last summer when my Auntie Myrtle came to stay with us, bang in the middle of the holidays. I knew straightaway that this was going to ruin everything. I told my mum and dad. They laughed. Rubbish, Auntie Myrtle was welcome, they said. Never a moment's trouble, my Auntie Myrtle.

But I was dead right. That Auntie Myrtle of mine was one big, fat load of trouble. The day after she landed on us, huffing, puffing and panting up the couple of steps to the front door, she collapsed. Crrrump! And there she was stretched out on the kitchen floor, looking just like a pink hippopotamus.

My dad knelt down beside her. At first I thought he might be going to kiss her. But no. He got up off his knees and said to my mum, ' 'Fraid she's a goner.'

'What's a 'goner', Dad?' I said.

'Never you mind, my lad. Just run along and play cricket with Jonathan for the rest of the day!'

Jonathan's in the class above me. He knows a lot of things. And he knew what

146

'goner' meant all right. He'd never seen one though. Only wished he'd been there when it happened to my Auntie Myrtle, he said.

Myrtle had never got herself married. And no wonder. She was too fat for anything and anybody. She used to waddle along the hall like a duck, cram the doorways and make the chairs creak and groan the minute she flopped into them. And eat! You should've seen the way she shovelled stuff into her mouth.

What a rush-around it must've been for my poor dad. Getting hold of a doctor to tell us Auntie Myrtle was dead — as if we didn't know by that time! Then my mum had to go looking for the vicar. And just as I got home from playing with Jonathan a white-faced man in a black suit arrived.

'What's he come for?' I said.

Mum clouted me across the ear.

'Shush, boy. He's come for your Auntie Myrtle.'

'Does he want her?'

'Yes.'

'Glad somebody does.'

'Shush!' I got a second clip across the ear. 'He's what you call 'the undertaker'!'

Sitting quiet after supper my mum suddenly jumped up.

'Fancy me forgetting!' she said.

'Forgetting what?' Dad said.

'Why, Myrtle's half-brother Harry!'

'The one in the middle of Africa?'

'Been there donkey's years. If he hasn't gone all native, I'm sure he'll want to be told. Maybe like to come over for the funeral. I wouldn't be a bit surprised. Remember those family picnics? Myrtle and Harry were always pretty close.'

Dad laughed.

'Well, close as they could get. Which wasn't all that close, being the size both of them were. I'll send him a cable.'

'Mum,' I said, 'What d'you mean 'gone all native'?'

'You'll see!'

'What will I see, Mum?'

'Listen, if somebody leaves England and goes to live in Africa for twenty-four years he's going to be very, very different from us. He'll be nearly African. It stands to reason, doesn't it, spending all your time among the tribes in remote jungles and rain forests and that?'

I couldn't get to sleep that night thinking about my Uncle Harry. I was so excited. I sort of fancied the idea of somebody going all native. Specially when it's your own uncle.

I could hardly wait to see this white man who'd turned into a black man with fuzzy hair, dressed in nothing but a loin cloth, squatting on our lounge carpet, eating a bowl of rice with chopsticks.

★ ★ ★

A wicked fantastic trip, it must've been for my uncle Harry. Coming all that way from the middle of Africa, carried by native bearers through jungles and swamps, riding on camels and elephants and on jumbo jets.

But then it turned out to be a sheer waste of money and effort.

Harry arrived too late for Auntie Myrtle's funeral. His taxi came belting up our drive about the time they'd be dropping my Auntie into her grave.

I'd been left at home with Mrs Next-door who had come in to help while Mum was at the cemetery. Funerals were no good for kids. I'd be seeing more than enough of them when I got a bit older, she told me. I was disappointed. Not so disappointed though as I was with my Uncle Harry from the jungles of middle Africa.

He talked just like our headmaster talks but posher. He didn't wear a loin cloth and he certainly didn't eat rice. He was nothing more than a very big white man in a tight grey suit, cream shirt and red-spotted tie.

149

Harry didn't look gone native one teeny little bit.

I could see all this the minute he stepped out of the taxi.

'Hullo, laddie. Am I holding things up?'

'N-no, Uncle Harry!'

'Don't tell me they've started. I came quick as I could.'

'I'm terribly sorry, Uncle Harry, but . . . '

'But what, boy, but what?!'

'I'm awfully sorry, uncle, but Auntie Myrtle left with the others about an hour ago. They'll be back any minute. Except Auntie Myrtle.'

'Damn! Oh dear. Extremely sorry about the language, laddie! I detest coarseness of all kinds. Tell me, how was your Aunt Myrtle looking?'

'Not too bad, uncle, considering.'

'Considering what?'

'The fall she had in the kitchen!'

'Bruised her fat bum, did she, laddie? Ah, ah! Tck, tck, there I go again. Coarse, coarse! A big girl, was she, your auntie?'

'Very big, uncle!'

'Bigger than me, laddie?'

'A little bit, uncle.'

'And when she bent over, did she . . . ?'

I'll never know what Harry was going to ask about Myrtle and bending over. Mrs Next-door suddenly appeared, offered Harry a cup of tea and showed him the way to the bathroom.

Harry had just finished washing his hands when they all arrived back from Myrtle's funeral. A pity she couldn't have joined us for that spread. She'd've loved every mouthful: cold beef, cold chicken, pork pies, chocolate sponge, sherry trifle and fresh fruit salad.

Everybody dived in like hungry, greedy pigs.

Everybody except my Uncle Harry. He just sat quiet, watching.

I didn't know where to put myself, as my mum might have said if she hadn't been too busy tucking into the spread with the rest. There was Harry all the way from the middle of African jungles and not gone native one little bit. And all these British people scoffing like wild farmyard animals.

'Please, please do have something to eat, uncle,' I said. 'You've come such a long way. You must be starving.'

'Very thoughtful of you but no thanks, laddie!'

'Is there nothing at all you fancy, uncle?'

'Nothing here, my boy, nothing.'

'Did you have a meal on the jumbo jet coming over?'

'No, but a good tuck-in just before I went aboard.'

151

'All that time ago? You must be feeling pretty hungry now then!'

'Yerss. But, as I said, nothing here takes my fancy. Remember, I've been out of the country for a long time. One's tastes tend to change in a different climate,' Harry said. 'Tell me again about your Auntie Myrtle, laddie. How was she really looking, hm?'

'Fat as I said.'

'Anything else?'

'Pink and red.'

'Hm, hm. Gee, I wish I hadn't missed that funeral.' My Uncle Harry frowned for a moment then he gave a slow smile. 'Could you tell me how to get to the cemetery?'

'Yes, uncle!'

'And d'you think I might borrow your dad's garden spade for half an hour?'

'Yes, of course, Uncle Harry.'

★ ★ ★

It was long after dark when Uncle Harry came back. He was all smiles as he marched up the drive, garden spade over his shoulder. His tight suit, not quite so clean-looking now, seemed tighter than ever. His red tie was missing and his shirt collar wide open.

He slumped into a chair, arms widespread. He reminded me of Auntie Myrtle and the way she used to flop on our chairs making them shiver and groan and creak.

'How good of you to make that long, long journey, Harry,' my mum said. 'What a shame you missed the funeral. Myrtle, I feel sure, would have waited if she'd known! So absolutely delighted you haven't gone all native. We didn't know quite what to expect. Now d'you fancy something?'

My Uncle Harry belched and at once he put a hand to his mouth.

'Oh, I do beg your pardon! That coarseness of mine surfacing again. No thanks, dear. No thanks. Quite honestly I don't think that I could manage another single bite!' he said.

Contact

She snipped the final thread and placed the crimson shorts over the back of a chair.

He nodded smiling approval.

'He'll be over the moon,' he said. 'He worships that pair of shorts. She bought them, y'know, the day she . . . Oh, sorry, love. I didn't mean to . . .'

'That's all right,' she said quickly. 'I — I don't mind.'

He embraced then kissed her. He would have kissed her a second time but she wriggled free to pick up some darning wool. She threaded a needle and, without looking at him, went on, 'D'you think I'll ever make real contact?'

'I've told you, it'll take time. Bound to. Nobody goes on living in the past, least of all youngsters.'

She shrugged and picked up a sock for darning. Drawing aside the net curtain, her husband peered into the backyard. In a patch of sunlight a boy was playing there.

'Look. Not a care in the world!'

He went out.

The boy was pushing a toy car through a

meagre pile of grey sand.

'Nice lot of sand there, son!'

The boy looked up. With careful, cupped hands he gathered together the grains scattered by the wheels of the toy.

The tone was accusing.

'Not such a very big lot.'

'Then we'll have to get some more, son.'

The young face lit up.

'When, Daddie, when?'

'Oh, soon, soon.'

'How soon?'

'Not very long. But you could have a day at the seaside whenever you like. Scarborough's got loads and loads of sand!'

'Tomorrow? Can we? Tomorrow?!'

'Y — e — s. Yes, why not?!'

'With you, Daddie?'

'' 'Fraid not. I have to be at work,' he said.

Disappointment at once seized the child's face.

'But Mummie will take you,' he went on.

'No, no. I won't, I won't. I won't ever. She's not my Mummie. She's not, she's not!'

The boy rubbed his eyes with savage, sandy fingers. 'She — is — not — my — Mummie. Not, not, not. MY MUMMIE

HAS GONE. GONE!'

The man wiped sand and tears away with a handkerchief.

'Come along, blow. Harder. And again. That's better, isn't it?'

'No!'

'Forgotten what I've told you? About two mummies? One in heaven and a new mummie here? Twice as many as other little boys!'

'I'm not going with her. Not, not, not!'

Once more he dried the child's eyes.

'Then you needn't, old son. You need not. So stop upsetting yourself. Build another sandcastle. Tomorrow we'll buy a tipper lorry. Tipper lorries are just the thing for sand.'

The boy resumed his game with the toy car, now a slow, half-hearted game. His father watched. In silence. Then he went indoors.

His wife was spreading a cloth on the table.

'Fancy taking him to Scarborough tomorrow, love? The weather forecast's pretty good.'

'I'd love it.' She paused, the table-cloth still unevenly spread. 'But would he go — with me?'

'He'll be fine — once he's on the way. I've dropped a broad hint and . . . .'

' . . . and he told you I wasn't his real Mum?!'

'Yes, but . . . '

She smoothed out creases in the now carefully centred cloth. 'A frightful battle, getting him ready,' she said.

His arm encircled her waist.

'You'll cope, love. Say nothing. Give him those crimson pants first thing tomorrow morning, take him for a walk — and end up at the railway station!'

★ ★ ★

They had reached the ticket barrier when the child slipped her hand. She turned in time to catch a glimpse of him as he thrust his way through the crowded booking hall.

'No, no. Come back. This way, dear!'

She tore after him. At the foot of Station Approach she caught up and clamped a hand on his shoulder.

'Wherever d'you think you're going?'

'Home!'

'What? Leave me all alone in this big station? You wouldn't do a thing like that, surely!'

'I'm going home.'

She bent to take the tear-stained face gently between her hands.

157

'Not to that little, little pile of sand in the yard?'

'Yes!'

'When you could have lots and lots of lovely golden sand on the beach — and bring back as much as we can carry?!'

'I — want — to — go — home!'

'Very well, lovie, we'll go home then. But before that shall we take a peep at the trains in the station? Not much good going home just yet. Daddie won't be there for ages and ages.'

He pondered, eyes intent on hers. Then, silently, he turned towards the station. They walked together. Steadfastly he ignored her outstretched hand.

Once more they reached the ticket barrier. As she was about to steer him through to the platform he stopped.

'Hurry, darling. You're holding up all these people who want to go to the seaside.'

'But we don't, do we?' He searched her face. 'We just want to look at trains — don't we?!'

'That's what we said. Look, a new shiny diesel over there. She'll be off very soon. Hurry, hurry!'

The ticket collector tapped impatiently, the crowd behind was pressing. The pair were thrust, willy-nilly, on to the platform.

Quickly she lifted him up and bundled him into the waiting train.

'I'm not going. Not with you. I'm not, I'm not. I — I can't. You're not my Mummie. Oh, please, I can't . . .'

Embarrassed by the curious looks from other passengers she gave him a kiss and turned his face to the carriage window.

'Look, look!'

'I — I want . . . I won't, no, I won't look!'

Out of his trouser pocket he dragged a new tipper lorry. He sat, tight-lipped, chin quivering as he turned the toy over and over.

As the train moved off he began to sob.

* * *

On the way from the station to the seafront he walked the kerbstones, keeping his distance from her.

'Well, how stupid,' she called to him, 'forgetting your bucket and spade!'

His eyes were firmly on the black line between paving stones and kerb.

'I don't want a bucket!'

'Then we'll get you a spade'.

She bought a spade, a red one.

'It matches your sail-cloth shorts,' she said.

'Very, very snappy!'

He stole a glance at his shorts then, snatching the spade, he fled, in tears, out of the shop.

'Damn, damn!' she muttered. 'Why ever did I have to say that?'

Clutching spade and tipper lorry, he was crawling under the railings of the promenade when she caught up with him.

'Couldn't you wait for Mummie?' she said, breathless.

There was bitter resentment in the toss of his head.

'You're not my Mummie. You're not, you're not!'

A man on a promenade seat gave them a curious look.

'They get a bit out of hand these days,' he said. 'Fancy shouting a thing like that.'

She forced a smile.

'Like what?'

'You're not his Mum, he said.'

'He's quite right, I'm not!' she said as she wormed herself under the railings.

The tide was high, the beach crowded and the sun extremely hot. From a deck-chair she watched him build a sandcastle with the new spade. He picked up a discarded paper flag and perched it at the summit of his castle. Then, with the flat of his hand he created a road spiralling from top to bottom, utterly oblivious of other children who paused to admire, he dragged the tipper lorry up and down, down and up the spiral roadway.

She heard a delighted chuckle. Drowsily she smiled to herself.

The sea was a long way off when she stirred. Instead of huddling together the crowds had dispersed over the wider stretch of sand. The crimson spade was there, thrust firmly into the top of the castle. So was the paper flag. But the boy and his tipper lorry had gone.

Scrambling out of her deck-chair she scanned the broad expanse of beach.

Pale blue tee-shirts, red shorts and yellow bathing trunks darted hither and thither in their bewildering hundreds. She grabbed her handbag and plunged across the wet sand.

'Have you seen a little boy in crimson shorts?'

Intent upon the remains of a crab the group of children seemed not to hear her.

'Have you, have you?!'

A dozen pairs of eyes focused on the boy who was examining the mechanics of a crab's claw. He wore red trousers.

'No, no, darker than that,' she said and she hurried on to an older boy plying a shrimp net in a rockpool.

161

'Have you seen a little boy in crimson shorts anywhere?'

'What's he like?'

'Oh, so high, fair hair and . . . '

'An electric motor launch?'

'No, no. A yellow tipper lorry.'

'Then I haven't,' the boy said, at once returning to the activity now in his net.

She skirted the rocks and almost fell over a woman struggling to support a child and dry its feet at the same time. Half a dozen more children clustered around, awaiting their turn with the towel.

'So sorry! Have you seen my little boy? White tee-shirt, crimson shorts. Very fair-haired.'

Face flushed by the exertion of drying feet the woman raised her head.

' 'Fraid not. But if you're just one kid short, take your pick.'

And the woman went on towelling sandy feet.

She scurried along the water's edge, from one end of the bay to the other, eyes all the time sweeping the wide expanse of sand. Here and there solitary figures dug furiously to capture the receding tide, others hunted for shells, others waded and splashed. But not one of them was wearing shorts of crimson sail-cloth.

Then, as if some giant vacuum cleaner were at work, the beach began to empty. She turned to make her way towards the promenade. A beach attendant retrieving and stacking deck-chairs had no time to answer her weary question. She glanced at the sandcastle, a flattened ruin. The paper flag, its staff broken, was still there. So was the crimson spade.

She stumbled up concrete steps to the promenade then, leaning against the railings, she emptied her shoes of sand.

A policeman was staring towards the horizon.

'I can't find my little boy anywhere!'

'Oh. What's he like?'

She told him, told him the child's age, his height, that he was wearing crimson shorts and had blond hair.

'He's got a toy lorry. It's yellow. And what makes things worse he's not really my own little boy.'

'Worse, madam?!'

'Well, you known what I mean. All that extra responsibility . . . '

'Not to worry, madam. It's happening all the time. Kids wander off without a thought. Then they're in a panic. Just like their mums — and aunties. There's a special place over there for lost youngsters.' He pointed along the promenade. 'Come on!'

She glimpsed a pair of crimson shorts. They were pegged to a clothes line. Then she saw the boy, wearing borrowed trousers.

He was the last child of the afternoon to be claimed. And he was in tears. She held high the red spade. He caught sight of her at once. Clutching the yellow tipper lorry he hurled himself from the lap of a weary municipal nurse.

'I — couldn't find you. I couldn't find you, anywhere — not anywhere, Mummie!' he said.

And he flung himself into her outstretched arms.

The Sand of Karilaa

The fingers of the old man drummed incessantly around the edges of the wooden tray held horizontal by a thin rope about his neck.

Trade had been flat as an empty water-skin on that long and dusty road to Karilaa.

'Religion and devotion nowhere near what they were in the old days,' the old man said.

Babu, squatting obediently at his feet, flicked a stone. It rebounded and struck the old man's leg.

'Clumsy child of black snake-pits!' the old man growled, cuffing Babu's ear. 'Nearly upset my tray. Lose our magic sand and even the miserable amount of trade still left will disappear like dew at dawn. And there'll not be one more rupee till the next Night of Pilgrimage.'

Babu rubbed a singing ear and he wiped his eyes with a grimy hand, all the time wishing he had flicked the stone a trifle harder. The old man might then have taken an enforced rest for a couple of days. What did Babu care if there was never again another Night of Pilgrimage?

If all the passing travellers believed so fervently in the mysteries of the holy city of Karilaa why were they wanting magic on the way as well?

Half a dozen times that wearisome day the old man had snarled instructions as fresh groups of pilgrims approached from the west.

'Sit you quiet as a mouse. Hunch up small. Hide one leg. Bend your arm — so. Keep on shaking. Eyes nowhere but to the dust!'

Babu had learned to be dutiful. The old man's arm was powerful, the knuckles exceedingly sharp.

Most pilgrims ignored the begging pair. The few who happened to pause were merely curious or simply glad of an excuse for a brief rest.

But now, almost for two hours, not one pilgrim had passed that way. The heat and quiet of noon were approaching. For the time being Babu could squat in peace.

Once, the boy's mind had sizzled with ambitions born when the white men came to build a bridge over the river. Outrageously they had flattered him. He knew where to find the freshest fruit and the coolest water. They promised to teach him how to read and write and how to build bridges of iron.

But those men, lightly forgetting, had built their own bridge and departed. All they had taught Babu was how to steal more efficiently and how to break a promise.

So there was no more fertile ground than Babu when the old man adopted him to beg and tell fortunes at the roadside.

In the distance a cloud of dust appeared, heralding the approach of more pilgrims bound for Karilaa's temples of devotion.

Babu, deep in dreams, failed to hear 'Boy, come closer. Down, down!'

Like a snake, the crook of the old man's stick curled around Babu's skinny leg, dragging him away from his idle scrapings in the roadside dust.

'Your good fortunes, oh, travellers on your way to the sacred city,' the old man whined as the group of pilgrims came by. 'Bide you a brief while and glimpse the wonders that can be yours for a miserable coin or two.'

The response was less than encouraging. All except one of the pilgrims laughed loud at the old man's invitation.

'Ah, wisest of travellers, most wonderful things I see for you, and only you, in our holy city of Karilaa,' the old man said. 'Pass your right hand over this tray and witness your fortune appearing in the magic sand.'

One bony hand held the tray steady as

167

the other prepared to move surreptitiously beneath it.

The traveller flung back his hood and, smiling broadly, made the passes over the tray and its scattering of dark grey sand. At once the fine powder formed into strange symbols.

'Behold, oh, pilgrim, some of the mighty things that await you in our most sacred of cities,' the old man said.

Babu raised his head and opened one eye. The traveller was a white man. A white man! White men were rich, so perhaps . . .

The stranger flung a coin into the tray of sand.

'A thousand blessings — and a thousand more if you could spare another for the crippled useless child, oh, master,' the beggar said, stirring Babu with his foot.

A second coin followed the first. The man took a further look at his fortune in the magic sand and then was gone to catch up with his more earnest companions.

When his benefactor was well beyond earshot, the old man again stirred Babu with his foot.

'Up, up, idle one. To the village at once and get me drink!'

Babu's limbs, from long crouching in the dust, were stiff. As he scrambled to his feet he lurched against the old man. The tray tilted. And every grain of that most magic sand of Karilaa slid away to mingle with the filth of the roadside.

'Clumsy little cockroach!'

For a moment Babu lay still, sobbing. Then he began to rake and scrape with finger tips, frantic to separate the valuable sand from the dirt and dust.

'Rake till your finger-ends drop off, child, but never, never will you recover my beautiful magic sand. Lost, lost forever. Nowhere in this world can I get more except in the city of Karilaa. So to Karilaa you will go. To a hut on the outskirts of the city where lives the one who works in metal. Give him this hard-earned coin for a bag of his best, most magic sand!'

The shouts of the old man grew fainter and fainter as Babu trudged, in the heat of the mid-day sun, the now-deserted road to Karilaa. But, as the cool of late afternoon approached, others appeared. Most were in groups, aboard ox-carts. Babu envied them their comfortable swaying progress. His eyes dwelt long and with longing on the fat skins of water which hung so temptingly from the rear of every passing cart.

By the time late afternoon had yielded to early evening, Babu's longing had given way to wild desperation. He fondled the knife concealed in his clothes as, in a ditch by the roadside, he lay in wait for the next ox-cart and its skins of fresh water. But Babu's wits were in no way as sharp as his knife. Although many a laden cart trundled by, Babu lay in deep, exhausted sleep and so heard nothing.

Then, roused by an ox-cart noisier than the rest, Babu crawled, stiff and chilled, out of the ditch. He scrambled to his feet and took a leap.

The cart was extremely ancient. It swayed like a drunken man.

Babu's knife missed the waterskins but the iron hoop of the wheel grazed his shin.

The child stumbled blindly on. A following ox-cart sent him sprawling. It, too, would have passed him by but one of the pilgrims, more wakeful than the rest, glimpsed Babu in the darkness.

'Stop, driver!'

The cart lurched to a halt and the other pilgrims aboard stirred to enquire what was amiss.

'See, a boy on the road!' the wakeful one said, leaning over the side to seize Babu by the ear.

'A boy? Whither goes such a small child at this hour of the night?' another pilgrim said.

'To — to Karilaa!' Babu said, terrified.

'To Karilaa? A child of your age? Devoutness indeed in one so young. The boy must ride with us to the sacred city!'

★ ★ ★

On the rough boards at the feet of the pilgrims Babu fell asleep. When he awoke he found himself looking into a face he had seen the previous day. The face of a white man heading for great good fortune in the sacred city, according to the message in the magic sand. The man returned Babu's stare and his face suddenly lit up.

'I remember you,' he said. 'What might be taking you to the city of Karilaa?'

'Sand,' Babu said.

'Sand? Why all the way to Karilaa for such ordinary stuff as sand?!'

Babu's reply was at once lost in the hubbub of excitement as the pilgrims caught their first glimpse of the temples of Karilaa, glinting in the sun of early morning.

The white man seized Babu's skinny shoulder.

'Ouch!'

The grip tightened.

'Ou-ou-ouch!!'

'What's so special about this Karilaa sand?'

Babu shook his head.

'I — I don't know.'

And he really didn't know. All that Babu knew was that there was no sand in all the world like the sand from the metal-worker on the outskirts of Karilaa city. And if he failed to get a bag of it quickly his ears would sing like the birds in the Karilaa trees for a fortnight.

Quickly the white man glanced at his companions. They had eyes and ears for nothing but the holy city.

So when Babu wormed his way to the rear of the cart the white man was close behind him. They leapt to the road and together they tore through the outskirts of Karilaa. The white man, anxious to visit the one who worked in metals, was postponing his journey of curiosity to the world-famous temples.

★ ★ ★

In due course it was discovered that Karilaa sand — or something very much like it — could be found in a vast number of places.

So now, in the white man's country, there is established a thriving toy factory.

Babu & White (Magic) PLC manufacture a shallow box bearing a lid of clear glass.

Inside the box there are iron filings. With the aid of a magnetic pencil supplied free with every outfit, even the most inexperienced of soothsayers can, by writing on the glass with that pencil, persuade the iron filings to jump around in extraordinary fashion. They jump even more smartly than the young technical director, Babu, used to jump in those bad old days on the Karilaa road.

Those iron filings create all manner of signs and portents. Not, by any stretch of the imagination, magic. Simply magnetic. A variation on an old scoundrel's technique where a grasping, bony hand secretly moved a magnet to and fro beneath a wooden begging tray.

And, so far as anybody knows, there is still an old scoundrel waiting and waiting for a bag of most magic sand on that hot and long and dusty road from the city of Karilaa.

173

Act of Revenge

The room lay at the end of a narrow and dimly-lit corridor. John paused and glanced up. High on the door there was a golden star. He smiled proudly to himself, tapped on a panel, and, without waiting for an invitation, he stepped inside.

For a moment he stood, dazzled. The dressing room was ablaze with light, its atmosphere heady with the scent of powder and perfume.

Merlinda, face close to the wide mirror over her dressing table, was putting the final touches to long, dark eyelashes. She caught a glimpse of John's reflection as he stood, entranced.

Through the mirror she gave him a bewitching smile.

'So glad you've come, darling!' she said.

John rushed across the room. He would have flung his arms about her but she turned to lift a restraining hand.

'No, darling, not just this minute. Undo all my hard work!'

She peered closely at herself in the mirror and deftly removed no more than an imaginary speck from her cheek.

'Sit over there and talk to me. Oh, it's all been so frightfully hectic. The most awful struggle with make-up and it's my curtain call any minute. What have you been doing with yourself this afternoon?'

John shrugged, his eye on Merlinda's dresser and the powder puff with which the woman was now delicately dusting the star's naked shoulders.

'Nothing much.'

He made no effort to conceal his bitter resentment that the dresser, little more than a stranger, could get so close to Merlinda while he had to sit like a good little fellow on the edge of a chair in a far corner of the room.

'Nothing much at all.'

Merlinda swished round on the dressing stool to face him.

'There, now. What d'you think?!'

She was the most beautiful creature he had ever set eyes on. He wanted to tell her so. But before he could utter a word there was an urgent knocking on the door.

'Two minutes, Miss Dubarry!'

Merlinda's face at once lit up.

'Thank you!'

She glanced quickly in John's direction.

'Time for you to go, darling. You know

175

where your seat is. Front row, next to centre aisle!'

For a second time he tried to kiss her. Gently, firmly, she kept him at arm's length.

'Forgetting my make-up again, darling!' she whispered, pursing her lips. 'Kisses later!'

★ ★ ★

On stage the first kiss came within three minutes of the curtain going up in act one.

Garry Dane, taking the part of a young man, an old flame of the character that Merlinda Dubarry was playing, has escaped from prison. Merlinda is the only person to whom Garry can safely turn for help while the hue and cry is on. She hides him from the police in her large and rambling manor house. Even her husband is not at first aware of the fugitive's presence under his roof.

Very soon the embers of an old love affair begin to redden and glow bright once more. Evening after evening the couple meet secretly in a summer house tucked away in a quiet corner of the garden.

That first kiss on stage was significant. Its object was to show the way in which the plot would unfold. The intensity of it at once revealed to the audience that this was

176

no ordinary meeting between a man and a woman.

A love affair, shattered once by a chain of unhappy circumstances was about to begin all over again, this time with a new and even greater passion.

For John, however, in his front row seat in the stalls, that first kiss was equivalent to dragging barbed wire across raw flesh.

Merlinda, whose make-up would have to survive at least until the curtain fell on act one, clearly could not have cared less about the damage to her lipstick and powder in the lingering passion of that embrace, the first of many, from Garry Dane.

Yet, in her dressing-room earlier she had firmly rejected the merest peck on her neck from John, never mind the gentlest of touches on her lips.

As the first act was drawing to a close, Merlinda and Garry grew bolder, even careless. Now they were meeting in the drawing room. Their ever-increasing abandonment made that first kiss seem like the pat on the head from a friendly old nun.

Then, 'Quick, hide!' Merlinda whispered. 'Listen. My husband, I — I think. Oh, please, darling, — no, no, no . . . '

At once the protests were smothered by

177

Garry's demanding, searching lips.

She struggled to free herself from his embrace.

'No, no, please, darling . . .'

The packed theatre watched and waited, breathless.

John could stand the strain no longer.

He sprang from his seat. He dragged a pistol from his pocket.

'Stop it, stop it!'

The weapon quivered like a jelly as he struggled to take aim at the couple who had fallen into yet one more passionate embrace.

From its muzzle a jet of water shot across the footlights.

'You stop kissing my Mum like that or I'll go and fetch my Dad!'

The Recipe

The rope of jungle creeper savaged deep into the muscles of Pascoe's neck. The sun had raised vast blisters all over his naked body. Yet, in its rare moments of lucidity, his mind kept on stumbling back to the crazy night that he and Maxwell had spent in the fairground at Manaos.

'Come on,' Maxwell had said, the evening before they were due to set out on their expedition up the Amazon. 'How about a binge? Last chance to hit the high spots for maybe a year — or even two!'

Pascoe had been less than enthusiastic. There were still many loose ends to be tied up before the expedition could get under way. But, at length, caught up in Maxwell's infectious gaiety, Pascoe agreed to that night on the town. And they had rounded off their celebrations in a Manaos fairground.

They sampled everything: the whip, the roller-coaster, the fortune-teller, the coconut shy, then the rifle range.

'Luscious cuddly blondes!' Maxwell said, pointing to a shelf of prizes, a range of flaxen-haired dolls. 'If I win we'll share.'

'Thanks but I always find my own women,' Pascoe said as he, like Maxwell, scored a bull.

Clutching their blond dolls they then strolled into the tent of the laughing mirrors.

Maxwell paused in front of the longest mirror. Edge-on it was shaped like a switchback. He stretched himself tall and the reflection of his head parted from his elongated trunk. He bent at the knee and his head slipped back into place.

'Absolutely painless!' he said.

Pascoe tapped his wrist watch.

'Waste of time. Let's go.' And, as they left the fairground, he added, 'Hope it's not some kind of omen.'

'Meaning what?'

'You look a whole heap better with something sprouting out of that torso of yours.'

Maxwell fingered his thick muscular neck. He laughed.

'It could stand a fair amount of hacking,' he said.

★ ★ ★

Barely a month later, now lashed to a tree like Pascoe, deep in an Amazonian jungle, head drooping, body limp against his bonds, Maxwell did not look as though he would ever laugh again.

Pascoe braced himself afresh. The creeper bit ever more savagely into his flesh. Tongue and mouth and throat were like dry hot sand.

'Must — must hold on,' he muttered, coughing at the effort demanded. 'Think about something positive. Anything, Maxwell, think about Maxwell!'

He battled to focus on his companion's naked and blistered chest. If the poor devil was breathing it did not appear so. But maybe his eyes were playing tricks. Every half hour since dawn their captors had dragged each of them round so that they constantly faced the sun's tropical ferocity.

'Blind and part-roasted, ready for the late night knees-up,' Pascoe muttered.

He strained at his bonds, frantic to get even an inch closer to his companion.

'Maxwell!'

Not a muscle in Maxwell's limp body stirred.

'Maxwell, Maxwell!!!'

Blood trickled from the wounds created by rope that bound Pascoe tight as the wrappings of an Egyptian mummy.

'Oh, my God . . . '

He must talk to somebody! Shout for help? Help?! The ghost of a smile seized Pascoe's swollen, blistered lips. A thousand miles from any sort of civilised community. Who could possibly come to their aid now? Not the flimsiest hope their bearers might creep back. The poor devils had fled for their lives when he and Maxwell had been taken prisoner. He couldn't blame them. The expedition had been fortunate to find any sort of native labour. The bearers knew precisely the sort of treatment that head-hunters meted out to their captives — if those captives managed to survive the earlier stages of the ceremony.

Pascoe screamed.

'Maxwell! Why the hell are they piling it on? Why the hell can't we get it over?!'

From Maxwell there was no response.

Pascoe clenched his teeth. No need to be asking Maxwell questions. Pascoe already knew the answers. At dusk their captors would return, hundreds of them, crazy and drunk, clamouring for the ceremonial kill. And Pascoe knew something else. Neither Maxwell nor he would be permitted to die swiftly. The ropes, the thirst and the sunshine agony were only the beginning.

Pascoe's mind ceased even its moderate functioning. When he stumbled back to his senses again it was night-time, bone-chilling, coal-black.

Lights attacked his sun-seared eyes. The lights resolved into scores of flaming torches that bobbed and swirled between the trunks of the giant trees.

There was the sound of chanting that soared to a crescendo of screams. A rustle in the undergrowth and Pascoe's bonds no longer savaged his blistered body. He lay spread-eagled, gasping, on the hard baked earth.

But the respite was brief. Powerful, clawlike fingers laid hold of his neck. Pitched on a stretcher he was dragged at speed across the forest floor, his wide-flinging arms striking tree trunk after tree trunk.

'If — if I could get some life into these legs,' he muttered to the night, 'I'd — I'd make a bolt for it!'

But, as if to remind him that he was near-demented, that his muscles were now little more than jelly, an arm struck a tree yet again and was hurled back to flop over his half-open mouth.

'M-Maxwell? Where the hell . . . ? Still alive? This — this could be something that's so far a very blank page about the Amazon.' The arm slid from his face to trail along the ground. 'And likely to remain blank. Not just a page, a whole chapter! Maxwell!!'

Tipped off the stretcher Pascoe lay, face down, on the dry earth. Acrid smoke from torches attacked his nose and throat. His cough was rewarded by a kick in the face.

He urged his head to one side. He seemed to be under cover. The atmosphere was stifling, foul. His eyes, ravaged by their long day under a pitiless sun, struggled to adapt to the gentle light of torches.

A picture of a low-roofed hut began to take shape. In the centre, on a stool, a daubed savage was sitting. Except for a headdress, as bizarre and colourful as the gew-gaw stall in that Manaos fairground, the man was completely naked. Balanced across his knees were two curved knives, blades glinting in the light of the torches. The chief, Pascoe decided.

'One knife, one victim. So Maxwell somewhere!' he muttered.

Already Pascoe could sense the razor-like thrust. The brief jagged agony at the top of the vertebrae.

The oblivion.

Unless, of course, these two-legged beasts of the Amazonian jungle had perfected a way to resuscitate their victims for a whole series of final thrusts.

Pascoe eased his head to one side.

Maxwell! Lying on a stretcher. Now they were propping him up. His chin was buried deep in his chest, his eyes seemed tight closed.

Gently, one of the daubed and naked savages raised Maxwell's head to dribble some liquid between swollen lips. Pascoe groaned. A crude wooden beaker was at once thrust to his own lips. Seizing it, Pascoe drained the contents in one wild gulp.

Almost at once the granite-like earth where he lay became as soft and yielding as a bed of feathers. He rolled on to his back. Gingerly he moved an arm. Then the other. He straightened both legs. The withering pains had disappeared. And his vision was now sharp as the two knives, his mind clear as crystal.

The liquid seemed to have worked miracles on Maxwell also. Raised on one elbow, he was now holding earnest conversation with the chief whose gew-gaw headdress was shaking with excitement. As if to emphasise points. Maxwell from time to time jabbed a stiff forefinger at the dark features. The rest of the savages watched in silence, nudging each other and grinning.

Desperate to hear the conversation. Pascoe craned forward but Maxwell had now dropped his voice to an urgent, confidential whisper. Pascoe could not hear a single word. But it was clear from the agitated movement of the headdress that Maxwell was spinning a damn good yarn, he decided.

Pascoe turned his head to survey his surroundings. Tied to the walls of the hut were objects that resembled coconuts. He leaned forward for a closer inspection. The objects were not coconuts. They were tiny heads. Shrunken human heads, mouths tight-lipped, faces devoid of expression, eyelids flat and closed, the hair framing each face resembled long dead grass.

The euphoric effects of the liquor at once drained away. After the final treatment, he and Maxwell, without doubt, would be joining the collection on the wall.

Slowly the man in the headdress rose from his stool.

'Hell, this is it!' Pascoe murmured.

But it wasn't.

The pair of knives clattered, unheeded, to the floor.

Maxwell was now jabbering at breakneck speed. The chief dropped to one knee beside the stretcher. Maxwell, suddenly silent, shook his head.

'Blasted idiot. What's he playing at?!'

Maxwell remained silent. Calmly he placed both hands behind his head and lay back to contemplate the roof of the hut. Then he gave an almost imperceptible nod.

The chief rasped an order and one of his followers handed over two objects that, in the flickering light of the torches, resembled yellow coconuts.

A second order and a dozen pair of hands gently raised Maxwell to a sitting position. Pascoe looked on, mouth wide open.

Tilting his head to the left, Maxwell thrust forward a stiff left arm. He bent his right arm so that the hand with forefinger crooked, the other fingers clenched, rested firmly against his jaw.

Roaring with mirth and slapping his bare thighs, the chief followed clumsy suit.

* * *

The final treatment was vastly different from Pascoe's earlier expectations. It was the Upper Amazon equivalent of the red carpet and it continued throughout the night, all next day and far into the following night.

When, at length, Maxwell and Pascoe set out on their journey back to base, their notebooks overflowed with information about Amazonian tribal customs hitherto never revealed to the outside world. And to smooth their way through the jungle the chief provided food and bearers and scouts.

Throughout their arduous and lengthy trek Maxwell refused point-blank to offer any explanation for their escape from further torture and inevitable death. His only response to Pascoe's persistent questioning was 'Wait till we're on our own!'

When within sight of a substantial settlement on the banks of the Amazon, their native escort disappeared, but not before the savage in charge, laughing gleefully, thrust out a left arm, crooked the other and pressed the hand to his jaw then gave Maxwell a knowing wink.

'What's all that about? And how precisely did you extricate us from that pickle?' Pascoe said.

Maxwell grinned in the way he once grinned in front of a crazy mirror in the Manaos fairground.

'Handed on the recipe,' he said.

'What recipe?'

'About the best kind of heads. A godsend they came adrift so easily.'

'What the hell are you blabbering about?'

'Never in all their lives had they come across heads like the head they nicked from our kits. Such beautiful golden tresses. Such fantastic skin preservation.'

'You trying to tell me they were taken in by . . . ?'

'Listen. Those jungle apes plan a full scale expedition to Manaos. Straight for the shooting gallery and the blond dollies. Only hope the proprietor hasn't meantime switched to teddy bears!'

189

Snappy Alibi

I was spending a cosy Thursday evening with Judy. The doorbell rang. A couple of coppers. Could I help with their enquiries?

'Sorry,' I said, 'I don't know a thing. I wasn't there!'

'Your trademark all over it, son,' one of the cops said.

'I can explain, easy,' I said.

'Go on then!'

'Somebody following in the footsteps of the mastermind, so you can beat it back to the beat.'

I left the pair at the door. They followed me inside.

Judy glanced at the three of us in turn.

'Safe-cracking!' one of the cops said.

Judy's voice was soft, silky.

'When?'

'Saturday.'

'Last?'

'Yes.'

'What time?'

'Between two and four in the afternoon.'

Judy smiled sweetly.

'Couldn't have been him then. We took a

trip to Scarborough together.'

'Proof?' the coppers snarled in unison.

Judy dragged a photograph from her handbag. One of those walky-snaps, prints ready-for-collection-in-two-hours style at the Happy-pix kiosk on Sandside.

'Doesn't prove much. All it says is you and him were strolling arm in arm along some promenade . . .'

Judy's voice was soft as ever.

'Some promenade?!'

'Okay, Scarborough promenade one sunny day!'

I snatched the photograph from the copper. The man was right. The picture didn't prove all that much. Sunny promenade, tide covering the beach, me, my jacket open, folded newspaper in its pocket, Judy on my arm, her blond hair caught by the sea breeze . . .

'Well, what more d'you guys want?'

Judy stepped in quickly.

'In a couple of days they can have the lot!' she said.

The coppers exchanged glances. It was pretty clear they hadn't a great deal to work on. Except a hunch and all that past record of mine.

'Okay,' one of them said. 'Two days for a stonewall alibi!'

The woman in the kiosk on Scarborough's Sandside said she could easily find out when the snap was taken. We could have an enlargement, big as a double-decker bus if we liked, the date stamped on the back. And she promised to post the picture next morning. Scarborough Town Hall was equally helpful. Certainly their publicity department kept a precise record of sunshine hours at the resort. But the man was a bit cagey about the Saturday afternoon in question. Not the best of days for advertising a seaside resort, he had to admit.

But when Judy came sailing down the town hall steps she was waving two certificates issued by Scarborough Borough Council. One was a confession about a miserable sunshine quota that important Saturday — only half past one until four o'clock, high tide a quarter to three, gentle breeze from the sea. The other certificate, in a few grudging words, mentioned torrential, unceasing rain the following days: Sunday, Monday, Tuesday Wednesday and Thursday.

We called at the cop shop. The cops couldn't argue about the Scarborough certificates but 'Well, that date stamp on the back of the blown-up picture could be a fiddle.'

'Then how about the newspaper in my

boy-friend's pocket?' Judy said. 'Headlines big enough, clear enough and simple enough for even thickies like coppers to read.'

The cop studied the picture.

'No day!' he said as if unearthing an enormous secret.

'Okay,' Judy said. 'You're a good reader, I can tell. Read the headlines.'

The copper frowned.

'All I can see is B O U N then D E R A then F E A R.'

'Listen, copper, carefully. If you could buy an unfolded copy of that Saturday newspaper you'd see the lot, wouldn't you, right?'

'Right!'

'Lend me your note pad.'

On the pad Judy quickly printed.

SOUTH BOUND HOLIDAY
TRAIN DERAILED
SEVEN FEARED DEAD

With lipstick Judy underlined BOUN of the word SOUTHBOUND on the first line, DERA of the word DERAILED on the second line and FEAR of the word FEARED on the last line.

'Now,' Judy went on, 'that train was derailed about 8 am that Saturday. The crash hit the headlines of the first edition, lunchtime.'

'The newspaper in his pocket could have been a day or more old,' the copper said.

'With both of us looking like drowning ducks?!'

'What d'you mean?'

'Next day, Sunday, raining cats and dogs. Scarborough's town hall says so. Same on Monday, Tuesday, Wednesday, then Thursday, the day you and your mate kicked your way into my flat — didn't bother to wipe your boots — remember?'

The copper shrugged and laid aside his ballpoint.

'Stonewall, copper-bottomed alibi, mate?' I said.

'Reckon so.'

'Tell me something!'

'Why not?'

'Already planning to wreck my next cosy evening with Judy?'

'What d'you mean?'

'Struggling to pin that rail crash on me, cock!'

Bedside Manna

I wasn't all that delighted when the telephone rang. Nor was Julia. We were starting out on what promised to be a cosy evening in her new flat. Candles, wine and a lot more besides.

'Oh, let it ring!' Julia said, snuggling closer.

' 'Fraid I'll have to answer. I had to leave them your number. On emergency call.'

'Well, I'm your emergency tonight, darling!'

'Temptation maybe. But not emergency. I'll just have to take it. Warned you, didn't I? GP boy friends might not be all fun.'

I reached over the back of the settee and picked up the receiver. A woman answered my irritable 'Hullo?'

The voice and the name were new to me. The address, fortunately, was only two blocks away.

I picked up my bag, kissed Julia.

'More, lots more later — please!' I said.

'No need to beg!' she replied.

★ ★ ★

A maid answered the door bell.

'Please come in, sir. Mrs Martindale's waiting for you.'

The maid led me across a spacious, softly-lit entrance hall and tapped on a door.

'Dr Andrews, madam!'

A graceful, handsome woman of about fifty, holding out a heavily bejewelled hand, sailed over the sumptuous carpet to greet me.

'We've already met. The charity ball in the Grand last month,' the woman purred.

I hadn't the faintest recollection of the meeting but I nodded.

'Why call on me, Mrs Martindale? You're not one of my patients.'

Mrs Martindale was clearly well practised in bewitching smiles.

'Reputation, Dr Andrews. In the short time I've been here I've not needed medical attention. But now this sudden stabbing . . . ' She winced. A sapphire-ringed finger pointed in the direction of her heart.

I led Mrs Martindale to her gilded and satin-covered chaise-longue where I gave her a thorough examination.

Apart from a pulse-rate slightly above normal, she appeared to be in excellent health.

'I can find nothing wrong, Mrs Martindale.'

My new patient gave a deep sigh.

'Oh, I am so pleased. What a relief. How very kind of you to come so promptly. I'm justifiably nervous.'

'Any special reason?' I said, wondering if I might have overlooked some obscure symptom or other.

'All my three husbands were right as rain in the evening, then before breakfast next morning, in every case — dead!'

'I see not the slightest danger of that happening to you, Mrs Martindale. You've nothing to worry about, I assure you. Goodnight!'

I closed my bag. Before I could reach the door the woman had leapt from her chaise-longue with the agility of an Olympic athlete.

'Please, Dr Andrews, if I may, I'd like to become one of your regular patients. Private, of course. You'll send me your account, won't you?'

'Very well,' I said.

By this time Mrs Martindale had opened the door of her sideboard, the sort of costly, exquisite furniture that I hoped to own myself one day when my new practice was firmly established.

'A drink, doctor?'

The voice was soft, seductive.

I thought about Julia, waiting and alone in her cosy, candle-lit flat.

'No, thank you.'

But already there was a more than generous brandy in an outsize crystal goblet.

'My late husbands were extremely proud of their brandies. They always kept this sideboard well stocked with their favourite labels. And I've continued the tradition.'

I loved Julia. I also adored good brandy.

I took a sip.

'Superb. Your husbands were obviously men of very good taste.' I drained the goblet. 'Thank you, and goodnight!'

Mrs Martindale placed an urgent hand on my sleeve.

'Don't — don't you think you ought to prescribe me some medicine?'

I shrugged.

'Not really.'

'Please, doctor!'

'Well, if you wish, yes. A mild sedative, maybe. Send your maid to my surgery in the morning.'

Then I hurried back to Julia and the rest of that candle-lit evening which we completed together without further disturbance from the outside world.

★ ★ ★

The maid collected the medicine next day and Mrs Martindale telephoned me in the evening to say that the effects had been nothing less than magic.

The following evening, as I was planning to collect Julia for the theatre and supper afterwards, the woman telephoned me again. Please, please would I call as soon as possible?

This time Mrs Martindale answered the door herself. She was dazzling.

'Now you're not telling me you're ill again, Mrs Martindale?!'

'No, no. Your medicine. It's — it's fantastic. I simply had to let you know personally. The telephone, even a letter, seemed thoroughly inadequate. And, you, you naughty man, I have to remind you — I've not had your bill yet!'

'In due course, Mrs Martindale!'

I was on the point of leaving after my second goblet of brandy when she whispered into my ear, 'Dare I suggest it? I — I'd love you to join me for dinner tomorrow, doctor. Just the two of us.'

'Thank you, Mrs Martindale. I'm sorry, I can't ... '

'Please, please, Dr Andrews!'

'I truly am sorry but for weeks and weeks ahead I'm frantically busy. This is a new practice. All sorts of problems still to be ironed out.'

Mrs Martindale was on the verge of tears.

'No — no hope, then?'

I shook my head.

'I understand. But you will let me have some more of that wonderful medicine, won't you, dear Dr Andrews?'

'Of course, Mrs Martindale!'

The effect of all that brandy was devastating. I kissed Mrs Martindale — almost. Then hurried away to find Julia.

* * *

Mrs Martindale's telephone calls, her brandy in crystal goblets, her invitations that became ever more pressing developed into regular features of my practice. Other regular features were the bottles of coloured and sweetened water which I dispensed with careful frequency for her phantom illnesses.

The bigger the monthly accounts I sent to her, the more swiftly they were settled. My bank balance began to soar.

At first Julia joked about me and the wealthy, glamorous Mrs Martindale. She used to refer to her as my 'gift from heaven' or my 'bedside manna'.

Then one day when it was utterly

impossible for me to escape from a brief afternoon tea with Mrs Martindale — she claimed that I'd forgotten to charge for at least two lots of medicine and insisted on seeing me to clarify the matter — Julia read the riot act.

Either we arranged the wedding day at once or she would start looking around for a steady line in chartered accountants or bank managers to share the cosy exclusive parties in her flat.

Following the announcement of my engagement to Julia, there were weeks of silence from Mrs Martindale. Until the day before the wedding. Then I received a letter.

'You are blind, you are heartless, you are ungracious, you are most ungrateful. With my experiences of three husbands already, I would have made you a wonderful loving wife.' The letter continued in this vein for several pages then — 'But, in spite of everything, I feel duty bound to give you a wedding present, dear Dr Andrews. So often you have admired my sideboard. With all its contents it is now yours!'

At once Julia slid a hand into mine.

'Want to change your mind, darling?!'

'What? And see you in the arms of some dreary bank manager? Not likely. Think of the house-warming with the contents of that sideboard!'

★ ★ ★

We did not invite any of our friends for the house-warming the day that the sideboard arrived. Six men staggered in with it. I'd forgotten all about the friends. But that's what can happen when you've married a girl like Julia. With incomparable and unlimited brandy in prospect.

I hadn't forgotten Mrs Martindale though. Particularly when I unlocked and opened the door of that exquisite sideboard.

Although it was crammed with bottles, there wasn't so much as a whiff of Martindale brandy.

That healthy, wealthy, thrice-widowed and loving Mrs Martindale, for whose imagined ailments I had been prescribing for months and months, had returned to me, intact, dozens and dozens and dozens of bottles of coloured sweetened water.

A Tide in the Affairs

There is no hard and fast rule. One man is destined for a broken heart when he is twenty-one, another when he is barely seven. The cause? Without exception, a female.

Apart from ensuring that Peter ate all his breakfast, apart from tying his shoe laces and ensuring that his coat was properly buttoned up, apart from taking him across the road, apart from giving him a farewell hug and a kiss, his mother did not want him any more. She was far too interested in Susan, a Susan born five months ago.

It happened to be one of those mornings. Although screaming at frequent and regular intervals throughout the night, Susan had been utterly incapable of explaining to her mother what was troubling her. And after no more than four hours of fitful cat-naps the same mother had to struggle out of bed to prepare Peter for school.

They were late. So late that Alan who always called for Peter at half past eight had been sent on his way alone. Then Peter, after a frantic dressing and breakfast, had been instructed to run as fast as his legs would carry him.

Halfway to school a shoe-lace thoughtlessly unfastened itself and Peter, as yet a tyro in the matter of making bows, was reduced to an uncomfortable hobble. By the time that he reached the school playground the place was deserted, morning prayers over, the first lesson already ten minutes old.

'Peter, what ever are you playing with under the desk?'

Promptly the boy abandoned the unequal and hopeless struggle with the loose shoe-lace.

'Er — nothing, miss.'

'Then pay attention. What was the question?'

'I — er — I don't remember, miss.'

'The question was 'How many miles to the moon?' '

'Er — three thousand, miss.'

'Nonsense!'

Peter flung a covert glance at the shoe now lying on the floor. What did he care about miles to the moon? He knew it wasn't just three thousand. But he wasn't thinking about the moon. What Peter had in mind was the United States of America. That's where he planned to go. Very soon. And not telling anybody, not even Alan.

A whole day of wrong answers and

inattention and consequent trouble dragged by and it was the sternest, most determined of young faces that accepted a mother's kiss when the boy reached home.

'An idea Peter's sickening for something,' Mother said later to Father, 'Point blank refused tea and disappeared to his bedroom.'

Father winked.

'An open-and-shut case of having a nose pushed out, dear. If I'm any judge of men that son of yours is suffering from baby-sister trouble,' he said as he folded his evening paper and made for the stairs.

'Hallo, old boy. Busy with geography homework?'

Peter glanced up, eyes brimming with tears. Going away wasn't going to be all that easy, leaving dad on his own. Even in the atlas it looked a long, long way across the Atlantic Ocean. He swallowed hard and, without appreciating that furtive acts by seven-year-olds are as blatant as a pair of bandaged thumbs, he swiftly wiped away the tears with his knuckles.

'Y-yes, geography.'

A hand, throbbing with comforting intentions, ruffled the boy's hair.

'We're in the same boat, you and I, old son. Both having trouble with girls. So, on Saturday, we're shooting off together.

Pictures, lashings of choc ices and a stroll round the harbour. And not a girl anywhere.'

Unhappily, Peter had not reached that stage in literature devoted to the study of Rabbie Burns. He knew not the first thing about the best-laid schemes of mice and men ganging aft agley. On Friday evening his father was driven to an early bed by a raging toothache and then, on Saturday morning, straight to the dentist's emergency chair. Yet, in spite of the agony, father made detailed arrangements for Auntie Muriel to step into his place.

The substitute outing with Auntie Muriel, although fulfilling in principle a father's promise, was an arrant failure. Aunts do not understand. The cowboy film at the Alhambra might be all noise, guns and killings whereas the natural history museum (where everything was already dead, a disappointed Peter noted) would be far more interesting.

Auntie Muriel took Peter willingly enough to the harbour but confessed to a total ignorance of maritime matters. She hadn't the vaguest idea how an iron ship managed to float, she was by no means sure how a ship found its way across the ocean when the land disappeared from view and, because one of the men from the lighthouse was wearing a uniform, she guessed he might be a naval officer or something.

'Now, I think we've seen just about everything, my dear. And it's all rather smelly and dirty. To be quite honest I prefer my fish with its head off, nicely grilled, on a plate. Time we went home to see your Mum and baby Susan.'

Baby Susan?! Peter didn't ever want to see baby Susan again. He'd had more than his fill of Susan. And of Susan's mother. He was making plans. Plans that would really work. Not like the plans of his father that didn't. All that pocket money saved in the red money box, a packet of chocolate biscuits and a can of orange squash from the fridge would be quite enough for Peter until the captain discovered him under the lifeboat cover. Maybe they'd put him in irons or set him to work peeling potatoes in the galley. But what would all that matter so long as he'd got safely away from England and that horrible baby Susan?

On the way home from the harbour, resolve faltered innumerable times. Leaving Dad was the main problem. But, as soon as they reached the house, that shaky resolve had hardened to irrevocable decision. Susan more demanding, more fractious than ever; father, after a painful parting from a tooth, gone to bed; Peter left in the capable hands of Auntie Muriel who, at six o'clock precisely, sent him upstairs to run his bathwater. Six o'clock! Yet ever since his last birthday his own mother had been letting him stay up until half-past.

While aunt and mother were arguing in the dining-room as to what exactly was wrong with Susan this time, Peter, before turning the bath-tap, slipped the fastening of the window on the landing. For even a seven-year-old pair of legs it was no more than a short jump from that window to the roof of the potting shed. And as Peter and Alan often climbed to its roof from the garden it wasn't going to be any problem climbing down when the chosen moment arrived.

Lady Luck was Peter's true friend that evening. Father's nightly round of fastening windows, sliding bolts and turning keys fell victim to the blandishment of hot milk, whisky and aspirin. And as a really true friend, Lady Luck remained with Peter. Revelling in the deepest and most restful sleep since the night five months ago when Susan yelled her way into the world, neither Father nor Mother heard the unfastened window fretting against its frame in the eleven o'clock breeze.

Close on midnight, the restless window — Lady Luck once more to be thanked — roused Peter. With a speed and efficiency that would have amazed his mother, he dressed, then tip-toed to the landing, down the stairs, along the hall and into the kitchen.

Leave a letter on the kitchen table to say that he had gone and might come home again when he was grown up? No, give them all a terrific shock when they received a post card with a New York stamp. Let them worry and worry and worry for days and years.

The unbuttoned coat, the can of orange juice in the pocket thumping against his thigh, a pair of shoes with loose laces that threatened to trip him up at every step and a heart beating like a steam hammer all added up to an infuriating hindrance on the way to the United States of America.

The harbour, at half past midnight was not in the least like its daytime, busy self. A light here and there, the smell of fish, of oil, not a sound, nobody, not even a coastguard or a customs officer. And one sudden, insoluble problem. How was Peter to pick out a ship in the dark that would very soon be casting off for a voyage to the other side of the Atlantic Ocean?

The night air was chill and damp. Peter

began to shiver. If he couldn't find a ship anywhere that was ready to sail to New York would that escape window on the landing at — at home still be open? Was — was Mother dabbing her eyes with a handkerchief? Was . . . ? Peter stiffened. In the darkness the clump — clump-clump of rubber thigh boots.

Peter retreated quietly into the shadows as Thigh-boots, a huge bundle on his shoulders, strode by and made his way along the quay towards one of the fishing trawlers dragging impatiently at its moorings on the turning tide. Thigh-boots flung his bundle to the deck of the trawler then strode on.

That was it. That was the ship. They were beginning to load her up now.

When he could no longer hear Thigh-boots, Peter glanced quickly about him to ensure that more thigh boots were not on the way, then tip-toed in the direction of the trawler.

Clutching the can of orange squash in his pocket, he scrambled over the gunwale and stumbled towards the bows of the vessel, not only the most nervous stowaway in the business but one of the noisiest too. Why, oh, why hadn't he remembered to wear his sandals with the buckles instead of those silly tie-up shoes?! He was very clever at fastening

210

buckles. He had been fastening buckles since that Susan came into the house.

A coil of rope and a black tarpaulin were pillow and blanket for the boy as he settled down to await departure. The rope pillow was hard and damp, the tarpaulin stiff and heavy but a stowaway revels in the hard life. He becomes thoroughly accustomed to the smell of tar and rusty salt-water after he's been at sea for a week or two. And the captain might discover Peter only a few minutes after casting off and be sure to offer him a bunk in the spare cabin.

In spite of the rigours of an illegal seafarer's bed Peter quickly fell asleep. But a mattress of cold, damp steel decking is a far more effective alarm clock than a dozen restless baby Susans. By the time grey dawn began to creep up on the horizon the boy was wide awake. He was cold: far, far colder than the day in December when he'd slipped into the yachting pool. But, as yet, no uniformed captain had strolled along the deck to stir the stowaway with a negligent foot. Of course, the voyage could be finished. The ship was lying very, very still.

Peter wriggled free of his tarpaulin bedding and struggled to his feet. The vessel was lying alongside a high stone wall and there wasn't a captain or an ordinary sailor or even a cowboy anywhere to be seen.

He scaled a vertical metal ladder and reached the top of a quay. He looked about him. A bit like England, all this. But it couldn't be England after sailing for miles and miles through the night. No cowboys though, so neither was it New York.

Peter's geographical problems were resolved immediately the one and only native on the quay — apart from the boy himself — shouted in a familiar and thoroughly unmistakable tongue, 'Hi, young feller, is your name 'Peter'?'

A seven-year-old's knowledge of natural phenomena tends to be as sketchy as his knowledge of geography. Because of the substantial difference between high water and low water some mariners can enjoy an entirely different viewpoint without so much as loosening a single mooring rope.

'Y-yes, I'm Peter!'

'Then it's time you got yourself home,' the policeman said as he took Peter's willing hand.

As a rule, no parents welcome the sight of their stowaway sons returning home under police escort. But the two exceptions to the rule that early morning raced each other down the garden path. Mother, the winner, was the slightly more coherent of the pair.

'Peter, oh, Peter, where ever have you been? We thought your were lost. And so did your little sister Susan. She's been crying and crying for you all the night long!'

Ring of Confidence

I was the greatest, once. No other illusionist ever spirited away a camel then, a minute later, pointed to the beast standing patiently in the centre aisle of the upper circle. A similar stunt with a Centurion tank repeatedly astounded and confounded audiences all over Britain and from east coast to west coast of the United States.

The only trick that ever went sadly awry was the episode with Susie Wayne. Since the day I made Susie disappear, a whole miserable twelve months have crawled by with neither sight nor sound of the girl.

No, I hadn't sawn her in half. I hadn't locked her up in a cabinet. I hadn't used her to demonstrate my version of the Indian rope trick.

To a magician, or, for that matter, any kind of man, Susie was perfection, a dazzling honey-blonde. On stage, while the customers gaped at her vital statistics, any illusionist could have got away with murder.

Unlike my other stunts, Susie's disappearance was completely unrehearsed. And utterly unintended.

It happened the day after she'd promised to marry me.

We made immediate plans, no expense spared, starting with a trip to Amsterdam, there to make a choice from the finest range of rings that the Dutch jewellery trade had to offer.

A further reason for our expedition was the final negotiation with Amsterdam impresario van der Heyden for a tour of European theatres.

The ring, however, was an absolute priority. Susie chose platinum with a sapphire flanked by a pair of diamonds. It was everything she had ever dreamed of, she murmured to me. But it was slightly too big for that elegant third finger, left hand, of hers. So, arranging to collect later, we left it with the Amsterdam jeweller for alteration.

Susie went shopping alone next morning. I was to pick up the altered ring then go for lunch with van der Heyden. Susie would join us early in the afternoon.

The menu was superb. I chose somewhat exotically. Van der Heyden, going rapidly to flab, skipped all the delicacies in favour of a simple green salad.

'My magical friend,' he said, 'I can offer you a twenty-weeks contract that will supply enough money to keep you in idle luxury for the ensuing five years.'

I looked him straight in the eyes.

'Twenty weeks? Is that really the best you can offer?' I said.

Van der Heyden seemed surprised.

'Is that not enough?!' he said.

'Aren't you forgetting I'm the greatest? Well, that's the way I'm being billed in Britain and the USA.'

The Dutch impresario frowned.

'Oh, but . . . '

I shrugged as I rose slowly from the table.

'There's a flight back to Heathrow in fifty minutes . . . '

Van der Heyden seized my sleeve.

'Please, please sit down. Nothing hasty. I am sure we can come to some agreement. Indeed, we must. I am so very heavily committed. From our correspondence I felt so certain. My friends in Budapest, Berlin, Rome, Ankara, Paris — well, it would be more than a considerable embarrassment if you — if I . . . '

'There's still ample time for me to catch that flight!' I said.

The Dutchman toyed thoughtfully with his lettuce leaves, as yet scarcely touched.

Then, 'Oh, very well. One condition and then you can name your own terms.'

I eyed the Dutchman with open suspicion.

'What's the condition?' I said.

'Demonstrate for me just one illusion, a disappearing trick, completely and totally new, here and now!'

'Here, this very minute, you mean?' I said.

'Here and now!' van der Heyden said.

'But I have no assistant, no plants in the audience, no props!'

'Don't you keep telling me you are the greatest?!'

'Well, that's the way I'm billed,' I said, my mind racing. 'Suppose — suppose we make it — yes — an appearing, not a disappearing, trick!'

There was the smuggest of looks on the face of that Dutch impresario.

'Very well.'

'Take a peep between the second and third lettuce leaf on your plate,' I said.

Van der Heyden explored carefully with his fork.

And almost at once uncovered Susie's sapphire-and-diamond engagement ring.

'Fantastic! How ever . . . ?!'

I smiled.

'The greatest, yes?!'

'The greatest!'

He beckoned a waitress.

'Try this for size, my dear, will you? If it fits, it's yours!'

The girl, eyes wide, lips agape in disbelief, gazed at the ring already fitting snugly on her finger.

A roar of laughter burst from the Dutchman. 'Now, make it disappear!' he whispered to me.

And, of course, this had to be the precise moment when Susie arrived.

She couldn't help but catch a glimpse of her ring adorning the finger of an unknown waitress. She let out a scream of anguish tinged with horror and disgust.

Then she was gone.

A wicked smile crept slowly across van der Heyden's fat face.

'Not a bad disappearing act either,' he said. 'In fact, without putting too fine a point on it, one of our greatest ever, I'd say!'

Clancy & Co.

It didn't leave a great deal of room on the pavement when that mountain of a man Master Mariner James Clancy took a stroll along Dublin's O'Connell Street. But it wasn't O'Connell Street where initially I'd encountered Captain Jimmy Clancy.

I'd been sent to a quiet customs station a few miles south of Dublin: so quiet, it was said, that if they'd made up their minds to place me on the retired list, instead of moving me, the revenue wouldn't have suffered as much as all that.

My first month at that little harbour station was peaceful: nothing in the least complicated had come along, just a few fishing smacks or the odd merchantman seeking refuge when the Irish Sea was up to one of its tantrums.

But then Captain Clancy's battered old coaster began to pay us regular visits.

'Keep your eye on him,' the loungers on the quayside told me following Clancy's second visit. 'Cap'n Jimmy eats three the size of you before breakfast. Then starts looking round for more. Fell an ox, he could, with those fists of his. Specially if he's been on the bottle.'

'Not to worry,' I said, drawing myself up to my full five feet six inches. 'Master Mariner Clancy needn't get up to any tricks with me.'

And Clancy did not get up to any tricks. So far as his dealings with me were concerned he was as punctilious and polite as a Cunard commodore.

I grew to admire Clancy. A first-rate seaman he was, capable, almost, of turning about that ship of his in the space of a fivepenny piece. Not that I ever saw him perform the miracle. Clancy was never the man for stunts. But certainly there were occasions when he needle-pointed that coaster of his towards our harbour on coal-black nights through fog as thick as a goose-feather bed.

Precise as the old Greenwich time signal, were those trips by Clancy to Dieppe or Antwerp or Rotterdam and back. On Monday morning he'd be nosing into the Irish Sea, hearty guffaws over warnings of north-easters, force nine. Then, ten days later, to the hour, he'd be tying up on our quayside, cursing the stevedores who didn't think he was arriving so they had all scuttled home for a long breakfast.

As for attempts at smuggling, you could have imagined that James Clancy was head of the Irish customs service itself. Even on the occasions when he'd brought trifles, a leather watch strap, for example, from Rotterdam, they would be laid out on the saloon table for my inspection and payment of any duty.

'Same old watch, you see,' he'd said, 'just the new strap.'

There were other things, apart from cargo, brought from the continent by Clancy. They were mainly items for his wife: wispy, delicate, silky creations that hadn't sufficient about them to keep a baby periwinkle warm. But the size and the weight of those articles had no bearing on the price.

'Are you sure that was the price, Cap'n?' I said to Clancy when he produced a gossamer sort of gown that I could have almost crumpled up in one fist. 'Nearly as much as a month's salary!'

'It's the truth, Mr Customs Officer.'

'Then you must be the most indulgent husband in the whole of Ireland!'

'Indulgent?!'

'Spending a small fortune on that wife of yours.'

'Aha, you've got me all wrong, Mr Customs Wallah. The dress isn't my wife's — it's for my wife.'

'For her — but not for her?'

'Well, you see, that wife of mine and myself don't keep all our eggs in one battered old coaster. I run the ship, my little wife runs a shop, a dress shop.'

I laughed.

'Hardly a dress shop though, with dresses at a price like that.'

'How right you are. We call the place her 'gown salon'!'

In spite of these early and amiable contacts with Clancy those loungers on the quayside continued with their darkly muttered warnings.

* * *

I had been serving at that quiet customs station for about six months when Clancy's ship came pitching and rolling into harbour on one of the wildest mornings they had known there for many a year. I was standing on the quay as she came alongside.

'Hi, Mr Customs Man,' Clancy bellowed from the wheelhouse, 'a sick man aboard. I'd like him ashore fast!'

'Sure, sure, Cap'n!'

Before they had time to loop the first mooring rope over a bollard I had straddled the gunwale and landed on the deck.

'Who's your sick man?'

'The bos'n.'

'Wanting a doctor?'

'No thanks. We radioed a taxi for hospital. Look, there on the quay already.'

'Right,' I said. 'Give me a minute then you can get him ashore.'

By this time, two other members of the crew had led the bos'n on deck, head swathed in yards of bandage.

'Goodness, what ever happened?!'

'Need you ask, a sea like that coming at us all the way from Land's End? Pitched headlong into a bulkhead. Lucky to be alive. He won't be much longer though if you keep him hanging around!'

I skipped aside and the two men carried the sick bos'n to the waiting taxi.

'Swallowed that yarn of Clancy's, did you?' one of my quayside advisers said later. 'Bulkhead, my foot. Tell you something, Mr Customs Man, old Clancy himself was the bulkhead. Out on his monthly rampage again. Something to do with the new moon, they reckon.'

'Rubbish!' I said.

'You'll see, mister. My betting it'll be the mate's turn for a roughing up next trip.'

Whether it was a bulkhead or Clancy's fist that created the damage I didn't really know, or greatly care, provided that Clancy did not try pulling fast ones at the revenue's expense or aiming his punches at me.

Whatever it was that put the bos'n in hospital the damage cannot have been particularly serious. The man missed only one trip to the continent and there was nothing to show except a few strips of sticking plaster when he returned to the ship.

★ ★ ★

A month later and a taxi was waiting once more for Clancy's ship. The quayside forecasters were quite wrong. The mate was in splendid form. He was the first to greet me when I stepped aboard the coaster.

'More sick men?' I said.

'Only one. The engineer.'

'What's the trouble?'

'Both legs broken, the cap'n thinks.'

If the rumpus that the engineer was creating as they brought him on deck was any guide, you would have imagined that he was suffering from ten broken legs. From the waist to his toes he was splinted with broomsticks and swathed in more bandage than many a hospital keeps in its stock rooms.

'Kicking over the traces?' I said.

Clancy had now joined us.

'No laughing matter, mister. In agony, the man. Tumbled down the companionway. Clear him, please, will you, then join me below? One or two items in the saloon for the salon, aha!'

Once more there was no escape from the doubting Thomases on the quayside. They were waiting, winking, as I stepped ashore.

'Slipped down the companionway, did he? More like he was shoved after Clancy hit the bottle too hard.'

The quayside forecasts were not all that much adrift however. The next victim of Clancy's fists was, in fact, the mate. But the mate required no assistance to get him on deck and on to the quay. Arm in a sling, he almost ran down the gangplank immediately I had given him clearance.

But no taxi was waiting this time. Like a hurricane, Clancy burst from the wheelhouse. And at once I knew precisely what they meant about Clancy's being a very, very big man.

'Where's that taxi?' he roared.

'Not the faintest idea,' I said.

'Sent a radio message sixty minutes ago!' Clancy bellowed, elbowing me aside.

'Now don't get yourself so het up. If you ask me nicely, I could run the mate to hospital the moment I've examined your manifest and checked the stores,' I said.

'No, no thanks.' Clancy was at once his old charming self. 'No thanks. Maybe it'll do the man the world of good to kick his heels for half an hour.'

It was substantially more than half an hour that the mate spent kicking his heels waiting on the quayside. When I left the ship an hour later — Clancy had brought back for his salon what seemed to be a total week's production of a Parisian fashion house — the mate was pacing furiously up and down.

'No sign of your taxi yet, Mr Mate?'

'No!'

'Let me run you to hospital!' I said.

'No, no thanks,' the man said, turning abruptly away to resume his irritable pacing of the quay.

I was standing by the window of the customs watch-house when the taxi arrived. It was in a hurry. I sensed the mate's agony as the driver bundled the poor man into the back seat and slammed the door. And when that taxi swung round and tore back along the quay you would have thought that every hound of hell was on its tail.

I'm pleased that my car was facing the right way. This saved valuable seconds. I don't remember glancing even once at the speedometer. But I'll make a shrewd guess that the needle was hovering on the ninety mark as both vehicles hurtled past, but not through, the gates of the hospital.

Outside a shop in an elegant and peaceful backwater not very far from O'Connell Street, the taxi screeched to a halt. It was the sort of shop that a man would never dream of entering, unless his reasons were strictly business: window seductively illuminated, all soft pink and opal and creamy white. And in that window nothing for sale except an exquisite, diaphanous gown. I recognised the garment at once. It had cost Captain Jimmy Clancy about as much as my month's salary and I could have crumpled and contained it in one fist.

As I was strictly on business I made to go into the shop, only just managing to get one foot inside the door before they could lock me out. Thrusting inside, I made a dive for a door marked 'Fitting Room'. The mate was there, arm no longer in a sling.

'Arm much better, Mr Mate?'

I turned to a slim and raven-haired woman whose dainty foot was struggling madly to kick a pile of discarded bandages out of sight.

'Good evening, madam. I think, somehow, you must be Mrs James Clancy.'

'I am,' she said as loftily as she could manage, one foot in a deep tangle of bandage.

'Your shop, is it?'

'My salon!'

'Well, Mrs Clancy, I'm a revenue officer and I have very strong reasons for believing that on these premises there are certain items . . .'

The stock of Parisian creations in that Clancy salon was small but extremely choice. I knew them. I had met them all, over a period, in the saloon of Clancy's ship. But of a vast collection of other articles I failed to recognise even one. There were watches made in Switzerland, bottles of brandy from France, big cigars transhipped from Cuba and diamonds from Holland so breathtakingly beautiful that I was surprised the Dutch had been willing to sell, even to such a regular customer as the Irish master mariner James Clancy.

Amazing, isn't it, what you might get away with if you are prepared to suffer a regular series of broken arms, broken legs or even gentle bumps on the head provided, of course, that you can lay hands on a plentiful supply of broad bandages?

The Hands of the Potter

Dusk was creeping up on the lamp posts and, as if resenting the intrusion, their lights began to shine more brightly. It was early evening, the quiet time.

I thrust my way through the swing doors of the art gallery. At once the eyes of the uniformed attendant latched on to me.

'What, you here again? Still cracking on you're keen on the painting lark?'

I stood quite still saying nothing.

'Not a doss-house, think on.'

The man rose and fell on the toes of his black boots, reminding me of some pompous, overbearing policeman warning a child about stolen apples.

'Yes, yes, I know,' I said.

Carefully I assessed the distance between the brass buttons of his jacket and the edge of the upholstered bench that ran the length of the gallery. There was scarcely enough space for me to squeeze past.

'Near on closing time. I'll give you five minutes, not a second more!'

'That's all I want,' I said. 'Just five minutes.'

The man edged back a couple of grudging inches. I eased my way past him and hurried to the far end of the gallery.

My breathless haste served but little purpose. Where the canvas had hung for so long there was now only empty space, shades darker than the remainder of bare, surrounding wall.

The gallery attendant was now close behind me.

I went on staring at the oblong of dust.

'What — what's happened to it?' I said.

'What's happened to what?!'

'My picture,' I said.

'Your picture?!'

'Yes, mine!'

'Go on, you old fool. You never done no painting in your natural. Leastways nowt good enough for shoving up there.'

I turned to him.

'Please — please tell me what they've done with it!'

'Done with what?!'

'My picture!'

'What picture? There's hundreds.'

'You know. 'The Hands of the Potter'. A potter's wheel spinning round and round, a pair of hands forming and shaping the lump of wet clay.'

'Oh, that old daub! Can't you see? It's

230

gone.' The man was revelling in my bitter disappointment. He pursed his lips. His eyes roamed casually up and down and across the rest of the canvases. 'Yeh, that's what I said, gone! And not before time. The bloomin' old thing must've been stuck up there since the year dot.'

'They'll be putting it back though, won't they?'

'How the hell should I know? They get a fancy for changes now and then.'

'I hope they do!'

'What, get a fancy for a change?'

'No, no. Put the painting back where it belongs.'

Slowly I walked the length of the gallery and sat down close by the swing doors. The attendant followed. He eyed me up and down, from the top of my shabby trilby to the tips of my cracked and gaping shoes.

I jerked my head in the direction of the blank space at the other end of the gallery.

'D'you think there's any chance they'll hang it again?'

'What do I keep on telling you? How the hell should I know? Mebbe the thing's had it.'

'Had it? You mean they might never . . . ?'

'Mebbe never. Mebbe they'll burn it. Mebbe it's burnt already!'

'Burnt . . . ?'

On the wall facing me hung a Pancetto: a full-length portrait of some mediaeval Italian nobleman. Pancetto had a long, long way to go in the technique of painting hands. But, perhaps, he had not chosen the best kind of subject. In that portrait by Pancetto the hands seemed useless hands, utterly lacking in expression, hands which had never achieved more than raising a crystal goblet or, maybe, slapping the face of some serving wench because the wine was insufficiently chilled to please a noble palate.

The eyes of the gallery attendant had been idly following my own when, quite suddenly, he seized me by the scruff of the neck.

His roar was one of triumph.

'The penny's dropped. Got it! Hands in your pockets every time you come sloping in here.'

'I — I don't know what you mean!'

'You know what I mean all right, dad. Come on, out with it!'

'Out with what?!'

'The knife you've got covered up there. Hand it over. Quick!'

'Knife? But I . . . '

I battled frantically for breath as the grasp on my neck grew more savage.

'Always sidling in here at the last minute.

Casing the joint. Getting ready to nick a picture the minute my back's turned.'

'No, no. I swear . . . '

'Come on, come on. Hand it over!'

In one swift and powerful wrench he tore my arms away from the pockets of my raincoat.

And then he stared. Stared for a long, long time. Stared at the smooth stumps where once my hands used to be.

'The — the painter?!'

I shook my head.

'The . . . ?'

'Yes, the potter,' I said as I thrust with my elbows at the swing doors of the art gallery.

Outside dusk had finally yielded to darkness. The street lamps were clear and bright. It was still the quiet time of evening.

I had reached the corner when a hand descended on my shoulder. I flinched and turned. The art gallery attendant was flushed, breathless.

'I'm sorry, very sorry. I'll get 'em to put it back. Tomorrow. I promise!' he said.

The Pick-up

It was a day of disaster, the day I signed him on in Pontibario. But I wasn't to know. And I'd had little option. A deckhand, desperate for shore and women, had jumped ship the minute we tied up and I was frantic for a replacement.

The replacement wasn't black and he wasn't white. But what did the colour of a skin matter? All I'd been searching for in the dim-lit dives that skulk behind Pontibario's waterfront was an experienced sailorman. And that's what I thought I'd found.

At the very beginning I was far from impressed. He was hangdog, he was shabby, he was as scrawny as an alley cat. But, from what I could gather in the brief time left before we were due to cast off, it seemed as though he understood the workings of a tramp steamer much better than most. And, so he claimed, there wasn't an island or a harbour anywhere in the Caribbean that he didn't know like the back of his scrawny hand.

In fact, there seemed very little for me to get worried about. Except the most piddling thing. The ancient flintlock rammed firmly between his belt and the threadbare slacks.

'That shooter,' I said. We were aboard by this time, facing each other across the saloon table. 'It'll have to be stowed in the ship's safe. No firearms elsewhere in any ship I command. So hand it over!'

He placed a protective hand over the butt of the pistol and looked at me with wide innocent eyes.

'It don't fire bullets no more, cap'n,' he said.

I shook my head.

'A hard and fast rule. I don't have many aboard my ship. But that's one of them. No shooters. Never!'

Disappointment seized the gaunt features. He got up, shrugged and turned towards the saloon door.

'Me a lot sorry, sir, but . . . '

It was coming up to high water. We were due to cast off in thirty minutes. It was imperative I had this other deckhand.

I grabbed a skinny forearm.

'If the thing doesn't fire any more, why tote it around?'

He tapped the side of his nose and he winked. In that instant I was reminded of a child boasting about a favourite toy.

'Let me have a look,' I said glancing

urgently at the saloon clock.

With considerable reluctance, he dragged the flintlock from his belt and, keeping firm hold of the muzzle, he allowed me to inspect the butt and the trigger and the firing pin.

He had been quite right about the uselessness of the article as a gun. Seized up with rust it could never fire another shot.

'No bang-bang, cap'n?'

'You're dead right,' I said. 'No bang-bang. Okay, forget the shooter rule. I'll let you hang on to it.'

'Thank you, cap'n. Thank you very much, sir!'

'Right. Get yourself bedded down in the fo'c'sle,' I said, then, as he turned I glimpsed, through a gaping tear in his shirt, skin stretched tight across puny bones. 'And on the way poke your nose in the galley. Sure to be a stew or something on the go.'

★ ★ ★

Less than twenty four hours out of port and it was already obvious I'd backed a winner. Far from missing the deckie who'd jumped ship, I was damn glad he'd made himself scarce. The little brown man was worth a dozen of him. He seemed capable of turning a hand to almost anything. And the rest of

236

the crew weren't slow in taking advantage. For a start he handled all the laundry, such as it was: there's no dolling up like Rio dandies aboard a tramp steamer pottering through the sweating Caribbean. And when the stowage of the cargo groaned for a check-over, he was the man for the job, leaping around the holds like a grasshopper, heaving and pushing and pulling until the crates fitted together again like pieces of a three dimensional jigsaw.

In the engine room he was more than proficient with spanner and oil-can. Very soon he managed to sweet-talk his way to the bridge for a spell at the helm, frequently taking over without demur that worst period of all at the wheel, the graveyard watch.

I was careful, though, not to let him loose in the galley. Until the cook, griping about something that had been gnawing at his guts ever since we'd sailed out of Pontibario, took to his bunk one afternoon and announced that he was staying there indefinitely.

That little man from Pontibario turned out to be very, very cordon bleu. If I survive to be a hundred and fifty, I'm never likely to taste anything quite so delicious as the goodies he produced over the galley stove.

The cook, however, wasn't greatly impressed. When he eventually revived and returned to his store chest he found that within four days three months' supply of herbs had gone into the cooking pot.

It wasn't long before I noticed that, sleeping or waking, my pick-up from Pontibario rarely failed to keep the old flintlock securely jammed into his belt. On the few occasions when I did catch a glimpse of him with the weapon in his hand he never wielded it in the way I'd expect a man to wield a firearm.

The first occasion came the day that the cook took to his bunk. I was having more than second thoughts about entrusting our stomachs to my Pontibario pickup. At first, through the cloud of steam, he failed to see me. Grasping the flintlock by the barrel, he was waving it over the stew-pot like a magician waves his wand.

'Everything okay?' I said.

The ritual abruptly ceased.

'Ay, ay, cap'n. Us two do fine, fine!'

I laughed.

'You two?!'

I supposed he was trying to con me into believing the rusty old gun had some influence over the quality of the stew. Of course, that was nonsense. And yet, and yet, the memory of those stews even these thirty years on can still make my saliva glands move into overdrive.

The second time I spotted the flintlock parted from the belt was on the foredeck, one shimmering moonlight night.

Once more the man was clutching it by the muzzle and, with a steady, rhythmic waving, it seemed as though he was offering the old gun to the Caribbean moon. So utterly engrossed was he in the ritual that he neither heard nor caught sight of me. For minutes I watched then, keeping to the shadows, I tip-toed away.

Looking back, it isn't all that easy to decide who was to blame for the loss of my ship. Maybe I ought to shoulder at least some of the responsibility. I'd been growing slack, I suppose. The sort of thing that can so easily happen to a man who sails the tropics year in, year out, without a break. It could have been the fault of the cook, going sick as he did. The malady he picked up in some sleazy Pontibario joint he passed on to me and the rest of my crew.

The only one to escape the bug was my pick-up man. He sliced through the work of half a dozen seamen. When he wasn't hopping from one bunkside to another, tending the sick, he was swabbing decks or, stripped to the waist, wielding a highly competent spanner in the engine room or taking more than his fair share at the helm.

Pitching, tossing, sweating in my cabin, I was long past caring about ships, food, flintlocks or anything. Until the evening when the mate, looking more like a grey corpse than my chief officer, staggered in.

He had barely the strength to speak.

'Any idea of our course, cap'n?'

'Roughly — roughly northerly.'

' 'Roughly' is the right word. As near as dammit bang into the midst of the Dragon's Teeth!'

I managed to raise myself on one elbow.

'Dragon's Teeth?!'

Within seconds I was out of the bunk, stumbling, crawling along the alleyway to the wheelhouse.

The man from Pontibario was at the wheel, a crazy, lopsided grin on his face as his eyes swept from compass binnacle to a chart then back again.

'To hell with charts and compasses,' I said. 'Sharp lookout. Damn rocks all round us. Can't you see, man, can't you see? Oh, get the hell out of it!!'

I seized a scrawny shoulder.

He smiled at me, the smile of a trusting child.

'We do very okay, cap'n. Magic gun take

good, good care of ship.'

And at once, leaving the wheel to its own devices, both his hands sought the butt of the flintlock jammed in his belt.

'You — you bloody little ape!' My tongue struggled with 'Get yourself below!' but I was so weak no more words would come. For the best, no doubt. The alternative to the man-monkey at the helm was a wheel turning wild and free. The only other possible candidate was the chief engineer already doubling in the stokehold and groaning about rusty knives thrusting and turning in his guts.

But what the little man claimed was correct. We were, in fact, doing very okay. Somehow that loony deckhand had safely taken my ship through the midst of the Dragon's Teeth, blackest navigation hazard in the whole of the Caribbean. If there is a tougher job I know nothing about it. Unless it's battling to thread a fine needle with black cotton in a force-nine on a pitch dark winter's night in the Arctic.

I stumbled out of the wheelhouse and crawled aft. The Dragon's Teeth were now well astern of us.

I cannot recall finding my way back into my bunk but I have hazy recollections of my pick-up man and his efforts to force hot sweet fluid between my lips.

'Get — get back to the helm!' I spluttered. His tone was triumphant.

'Ay, ay, cap'n. Ay, ay!'

The Pontibario sickness ran its course, leaving its victims listless, feeble. If we hadn't been running such a long way behind schedule I'd have gladly given my crew a fortnight ashore to recuperate. But the pressure was on. In a desperate attempt to catch up, my ship was sailing into port on one tide, discharging her cargo, loading up and moving off next high water.

For a month this hell-for-leather rush went on, darting from one Caribbean island to the next, until our final run of the charter, a voyage south, back to Pontibario.

Far away and to starboard lay the coast of Venezuela. On our port side the waters of the Caribbean lapped the moonlit beaches of Trinidad. I had joined my pick-up man at the wheel. Once more we were close to the Dragon's Teeth.

'Hard aport — aport!' I said as the rocks loomed dead ahead, black against the shimmering swell.

He took not the slightest notice.

I grabbed the helm.

'APORT, APORT!'

The sickness had left me weak as skimmed and watered milk. Even against the puny grasp of my Pontibario pick-up I could shift the wheel scarce more than half an inch.

Within seconds we struck. For hideous dragged-out moments my ship rocked, stem to stern, like a giant see-saw. She then went very still.

Pitched by the impact against the panelling of the wheelhouse I struggled to my knees and crawled up the crazy tilt of the floor. At the foot of the compass binnacle my Pontibario man lay twisted and quiet. Close to his outstretched hand was the flintlock.

I hooked my fingers over the rim of the binnacle, hoisted myself up then leaned over the pick-up to grab his rusty old gun.

The needle of the compass twitched erratically then swung half a dozen points to east.

From port to starboard, forward and aft, I waved the ancient flintlock. Like any other magnet excited by the proximity of a chunk of steel, my ship's compass was dancing the merriest of carefree horn pipes.

And that is why it was such a day of black disaster, the day I signed on the little man in Pontibario.

And that is how we sailed so neatly — and luckily — through the Dragon's Teeth on our passage north.

And how we were not so lucky on that

final trip of our charter south.

And why that ship of mine, now a battered, rusty old hulk, sits high and dry on some rocks in the sweltering Caribbean.

The Safer Job

Mixed up with a woman again, was he?

She turned on the gas and momentarily forgot to strike a match.

With a shudder she remembered the last time, how he'd snarled when she questioned him, how he'd sneered when the affaire, after a few weeks, came to abrupt end. She ought to consider herself lucky he'd come back to her, he'd said. Very lucky! How did she imagine she'd be able to cope with no breadwinner around the place?

And because she hadn't quite known how she was going to manage on her own, she'd swallowed the remnants of her pride and taken him back.

But, she kept on telling herself, if the same thing ever happened again hc could clear out for good. She would go on living, somehow.

She glanced at the clock. He'd be home within the hour. After the long climb up Mariner Steps and his couple of pints at The Mariners Arms. Soon she would hear the squeak of the back door, the thud of his rubber thigh boots as he kicked them off, then the splash of the kitchen tap.

She knew precisely what his first words would be.

'My dinner ready?'

This, however hadn't been the way of things on Monday or yesterday. Although The Mariners Arms closed at three o'clock it had been long past five when he'd come home.

'What's taken him all of a sudden?' one of the fishermen had asked as she'd hurried along Mariner Row to the corner shop that morning.

'Taken him?'

The man's wink was bordering on the obscene.

'He's acting a lot different these days.'

She forced a smile.

'Maybe it's that new coble of his. Making him a bit uppish,' was her reply.

'He never seems to sup his pint in the bar these days. Always in the snug. Bit funny?'

Annoyance made her bold.

'Funny? Not in the least. A man can drink where he chooses,' she said as she seized the handle of the shop door.

'Where his fancy woman chooses, you mean. Take my tip, missus, keep your eye on them both.'

The tinkle of the shop bell saved her from

hearing any more of what she'd already heard from other doorstep gossipers in Mariner Row.

The potatoes were simmering gently. She peered from the window towards the fish quay far below. She couldn't quite single him out from the rest of the fishermen down there. But one particular figure wearing an apple-green blouse and tight cream ski-pants was only too distinct. The other woman. A red-head.

Savagely she drained the potatoes. She dragged on her coat, steeling herself for an attack on the pair of them in the snug at The Mariners Arms.

First, a piece of her mind to that red-head.

'Now then, what d'you think you're up to? Don't you know he's married? Or doesn't that sort of thing matter to the likes of you?'

Then, to her husband sitting there in silence, smirking maybe, 'Back at your old games, again, eh?'

Just the three of them in the snug, so safe enough to say precisely what she thought.

Safe enough? But would it be? What about the crowded bar next door? As they were downing their pints of beer, they'd all suddenly pause, glasses in mid-air, listening through the serving hatch, struggling to catch every word. And deep, deep down she was terrified about creating a scene. After all, she had some fragments of pride still left. In a tiny fishing village everybody knew far too much about everybody else already.

So — so, perhaps, after all, she wouldn't go out. Let things wait. She tore off her coat and began to set the table.

Once more it was long past five o'clock when her husband came home.

She glanced meaningfully at the clock.

'Late again.'

'So what?' he said.

'Meal ruined for the third time in a row.'

He shrugged.

'It'll do.'

'A good catch this morning?'

'Not bad.'

'Prices all right?'

'Fair,' he said.

'Spent up already?'

'No.'

She slid a plate in front of him. He ate quickly. She idled with her knife and fork. As soon as his plate was empty she snatched it up and went into the kitchen.

A moment later she put her head round the door.

'Come on, you'd better tell me. Who is it this time?'

He did not respond.

'I'm entitled to know,' she said as she came back into the living room.

'A woman I met.'

'A red-head? The one in tight ski-pants?'

He nodded.

'I didn't recognise her. Local is she?'

'No.'

She eyed him in silence. His attitude was a puzzle. When she'd stumbled upon his last affaire he'd been full of talk. Lies and hollow laughs and sneers. This time he wasn't saying a word. Curious!

He brushed roughly past her and went upstairs. She was about to start the washing-up when he re-appeared. He was dressed in his navy blue suit. He was wearing the tie she'd bought for his birthday.

'Where does this one come from?' she said.

'Mm? Oh, Leeds.'

'Down here for long?'

'Till Saturday.'

'Well, I hope you're not forgetting the last time!'

His laugh was cut short by the crash of the front door as it closed behind him.

In the midst of washing-up, she suddenly

grabbed her coat and dived into Mariner Row, struggling to thrust her arms into the sleeves as she ran. She took Mariner Steps two and three at a time until, panting and distraught, she reached the fish quay. The seagulls perched on the tangle of nets eyed her nervously as she made her way between the scatter of fish-boxes.

He'd be with that woman from Leeds. It was barely six o'clock so they wouldn't be in the snug at the Mariner Arms yet. But where, where?

A mooring-rope strung across her path brought her to an abrupt halt. Battling to regain breath, she collapsed on an upturned fish-box.

Where, where, where? Her eyes focused on, without seeing, the distant horizon.

She put a hand to her forehead.

Oh, all that hassle, the battle of bitter words, the misery of it all! She couldn't help but bring to mind the last time it happened.

So maybe, — maybe wait then until Saturday when it could be all over?

Thursday, Friday, Saturday. Just three more days.

She shot to her feet. No, no, no! For far too long she'd been the meek quivering little mouse.

She scurried down the concrete steps leading to the now deserted beach. She ran as fast as the yielding sand and the heels of her shoes would permit. High overhead, the kittiwakes soared and glided and swooped, seeming to cry, 'Keep away, keep away!'

'Keep away?' she called back to them. 'Precisely what that fancy woman of his from Leeds ought to be doing — keeping away!'

Why couldn't the trollop keep her hands off! Fine for her, on holiday, having fun, the affaire all but forgotten by Sunday morning. Then recalled as a seaside tale of whirlwind romance, suitably embroidered, at some suburban hen-party in the autumn.

She paused. Jealous? Was she jealous? Oh, no! Bitter and resentful maybe but not by any stretch of the imagination jealous. Not any more. After that previous affaire her love for him was as dry and as dead as the black seaweed scattered among the rocks above high water mark.

Yet somehow she'd managed to go on living under the same roof. She'd had to. He was, as he kept on snarling, the breadwinner.

She stumbled to the promenade and, hands deep in pockets, head down, she began to climb up Main Street. The occasional curtain was quickly dragged aside as she passed and just as quickly thrust back into place as she turned her head.

She was rounding the corner of Mariner Row when she came face to face with them. They were arm in arm. At once that woman from Leeds tightened her grasp on him. The pair eyed the unbuttoned coat, the apron she'd forgotten to take off, the wind-swept hair. The red-head grimaced. Her husband eyed her with icy disdain.

She knew precisely what she ought to have done. Hurled herself into the attack like a wounded tigress.

But, without so much as a word, she hastened past them and went stumbling blindly along Mariner Row.

⋆ ⋆ ⋆

That night, the bed-clothes firmly held to her chin, she was sitting up, watching the beam from the lighthouse sweeping the pattern of the wallpaper, when her husband came into the bedroom.

'Well?' she said.

He dragged off the silk tie and flung it on the dressing table.

'I'm off!' he said.

'Off? When?!'

'Saturday.'

'With her?'

'Yes.'

He was standing, black and motionless, against the intermittent flashes from the lighthouse.

'You know what you're doing, I suppose,' she said.

'Yes!'

'No creeping home when things don't work out.'

'They'll work out all right.'

'What about your new fishing boat and all your gear?'

'Flogging it all.'

'What happens when you want to go back to it?'

'I won't. She's finding me a job in Leeds.'

'What sort of job?'

'A safer job.'

'After the fishing game you wouldn't stand any other job five minutes.'

'Sick of the lot!'

'Not sick of women evidently.'

'This one's different.'

'So was the last one — for a week or two.'

'Shut up!'

'Well, all I can say is 'You must be crazy'!'

When she got up next morning she found the remains of his breakfast on the table.

On the way to the shop on the corner of Mariner Row she passed a neighbour sweeping the doorstep.

'Heard about him, I suppose?' the woman said.

'Heard what?'

'Him and his fancy woman.'

'Oh — oh, that! A cousin of his from Leeds here for a week or so.'

The woman smirked.

'A bit too close for cousins, them two. If I was you I wouldn't half be watching.'

★ ★ ★

She was preparing vegetables when he came home. He strode past her into the living room.

'Got rid,' he said.

'You fool. You'll be sorry.'

That night, and the next, he slept on the sofa downstairs. Early on Saturday morning he came into the bedroom.

'Getting my things,' he said.

She lay in bed, tight-lipped.

He rammed shirts and socks and underwear

254

into a suitcase. She watched. She said nothing. There was such a thing as pride and she was going to be in need of every ounce of pride she could muster. In Mariner Row, the shop at the corner, in the High Street, on the fish quay. Already she could hear the whispers.

'Mouse of a woman!'

'Hasn't the foggiest idea how to hold on to a man.'

Well, if they really wanted to know, she hadn't the faintest desire to hold on to him. It was good riddance. She'd show them. And him. She'd manage all right.

Her face now deep in the pillow, she heard him open yet another drawer in the tallboy.

She raised her head for a moment.

'Now don't forget. Once outside that door and I'm never, never taking you back,' she said.

And he'd gone when she raised her head a second time.

It was a frantically hectic summer. By the end of May the holidaymakers had begun to throng her tiny cottage. She squeezed a second bed into the front bedroom, a second bed and a cot into the spare room and, after a feverish cleaning and decorating, she converted the attic into a dormitory for three children. For herself there was nowhere to sleep except the sofa in the living room.

Not until chill morning mists began to herald autumn was she alone in her cottage again. By that time she had made enough money to see her comfortably through the winter and the spring, right to the doorstep of summer.

The policeman who called one evening in October was little more than a youth. Deeply embarrassed, he struggled desperately to fit the enormity of his task to the confines of permitted police jargon.

'Your husband's employers'll be writing,' he said.

'Why?'

'He's gone — he died.'

'Died?!'

'Got himself drowned.'

'Drowned? My husband? Never!'

'Well, that's the message.'

'Impossible!'

She snatched a glance at the string of fishing boats moored alongside the quay below.

'Him getting drowned? For twenty-five years he's been taking a fishing boat to sea. In all weathers, summer and winter alike. Never so much as a wet foot. Is this some sort of leg-pull? My husband? How ever d'you get yourself drowned in a

256

place like Leeds? It isn't possible!'

'You wouldn't've thought so,' the police-man said.

'You said something about employers. What was his job?'

'Don't you know?'

'Not the faintest idea.'

'Superintendent of boating on the park lakes.'

'Park lakes!'

She snatched another glance at the fish quay.

'So that was the safer job she landed him with. Boats on a park lake!!'

She began to laugh, wildly, hysterically.

And she was still laughing, perhaps now a trifle less wildly, a trifle less hysterically, as an embarrassed police constable hurried past the shop on the corner of Mariner Row.

Dropping the Pilot

On a night such as that nobody but an idiot would have wriggled out of the bedclothes. Unless he happened to be the solitary customs officer at an insignificant harbour a few miles south of Dublin. Like me, waiting for a ship to make port. A ship under the command of salty-tempered master mariner James Clancy.

The chips seemed all stacked against Clancy and his ship that night. Holding on to the handrail for dear life, I'd struggled up the look-out a dozen times to scan the black reaches of the January sea but never a glimmer of mast-head lights anywhere.

I telephoned the harbour pilot.

'Clancy's ship,' I said, 'You aiming to bring her in if she shows up?'

'A night like this, man? You must be mad. If Clancy hasn't the nous to heave-to till this lot blows over he can kick his heels out there till it does.'

'Fine, fine,' I said, 'So long as I know. Goodnight!'

Scarcely had I put the telephone back on its cradle when I heard a hooting and a tooting way out to sea that, in spite of the gale, would have made every corpse in the village churchyard cringe and groan then turn over on its side.

Once more I stumbled up the look-out.

'Hoo-hoo-hoo!' a distant ship moaned, then half a dozen lights began to flash.

Again I rang the pilot.

'Old Clancy out there, raising hell. You bringing him in?'

'I've already told you, mister. I — am — not. Jimmy Clancy stays out there till daybreak — or next Tuesday if the weather doesn't ease off a whole lot.'

'I can get my head down again, I suppose?' I said.

'Do as you like, same as me!' the pilot said.

I couldn't manage sleep. Every time my head dropped, the banshee wail from Clancy's ship brought it up with a jerk that threatened to dislocate my neck.

But maybe I did nod off eventually for, when next I glanced through the customs watch-house window, streaks of white and grey were slashing the night sky.

The gales had barely lost the edge of their fury. Our Irish sea bore a beaten, battered and pummelled look. Yet there was Clancy's ship aiming, somewhat erratically I thought, for the mouth of the harbour.

'So,' I said to myself, 'the pilot changed his mind. Took pity on old Clancy out there in the storm. And, so-ho, that rascal of a pilot hoped to pull a fast one on me, saying Clancy'd got to stay out there till the gale slackened off. Something fishy going on, I reckon!'

I rammed my uniform cap hard above my ears, quickly buttoned my mackintosh and sped for the quayside. Concealed by a wooden shack, I watched and waited for the vessel to berth.

The pilot, I decided, must have sneaked aboard and either been hitting the bottle for three or four hours with Jimmy Clancy or he was still half asleep. Never in all my maritime life had I seen anybody make such a hash of berthing a little ship. The waters of the harbour were not particularly rough: it was a south-westerly gale so the worst of it was blowing clean over our heads. Yet Clancy's ship was backing and filling, filling and backing, scraping the concrete quay then shying off again, like some lively colt quarrelling with a fence on an April afternoon.

The moment the ship moored I leapt aboard, ready to tell the pilot precisely what I thought about the way he'd tried to pull a fast one and how he ought to pack up his job for something else in the dark, growing mushrooms for instance.

' 'Morning, cap'n!' I called to Clancy on his bridge.

'Noisy wind kept you awake all night, Mr Customs Man?!'

'Not the wind, Cap'n Jim,' I said. 'All that hootin' and tootin' of yours wasn't exactly a soothing lullaby. I can't spot the pilot with you. Is he there?'

'Pilot?!' Clancy roared. 'The bilge rat refused to turn out.'

'So you brought the ship in yourself?!'

'Me and the engines, yes.'

'Well, come back all I've been thinking,' I said.

'What d'you mean?'

'I wasn't vastly impressed with the berthing tactics.'

'You weren't what?!'

'If it'd been the work of the pilot, I mean.'

'Tell you something, Mr Customs. For years I've been using the pilot round here. The shoals and the channels were tricky, they always said. Paying twenty-five punts in and twenty-five punts out. Never again, though. If I can berth my ship on my own in weather like this, I can berth her in any old conditions, any old time.'

'Using a pilot's a port regulation,' I said.

'Bubbles to your regulations. No more pilot fees out of me.'

I shrugged.

'Your business entirely, cap'n. Now, can we press on with mine?!'

★ ★ ★

That was the way Captain Clancy became his own pilot and saved himself money. The harbour pilot didn't altogether approve but he dearly loved his bed and, running the village store as well as piloting, he wasn't exactly a pauper. So he told Clancy that the regulations weren't really aimed at competent deck officers, the likes of Jimmy Clancy. And I heard he'd demanded ten punts for keeping out of the way and in bed. I also heard that Clancy settled for five punts with a promise of a bottle or two of duty-free brandy when nobody of importance happened to be watching.

For years there had been a steady trade in contraband at the harbour, I knew. Detection by a one-man band like mine was difficult. But Clancy's old coaster was the culprit, I felt quite sure. All other craft using the place rarely put in to foreign ports, apart from Liverpool or Holyhead. Using a quick system of barter with passing ships on the high seas, fishing vessels were no more than minor offenders. They might exchange a stone of fresh herring for some rum but by the time they made harbour the bottles would be upside down, empty.

★ ★ ★

My wife and I were taking a country drive one day when she suddenly demanded I find her some afternoon tea.

'But we're on the road to Ballyragget, my love,' I said. 'Not in the middle of O'Connell Street. Where, d'you imagine, I can find a tea shop around here?'

'You're the one who invited me out for the day,' she said, demonstrating her usual brand of logic.

Eventually, I pulled up at a tiny country inn where, to my surprise, they were only too pleased to supply afternoon tea.

'Steadyish trade?' I said to the landlord, replete.

'For teas, sir, yes. For liquor, the hard stuff, no.'

'Too expensive?' I said.

'Sure it is, sir, when they can buy every drop for next to nothing down on the coast.'

'Is that so?' I said.

'It is damn so, sir!'

'Very annoying, very interesting,' I said as I settled the modest bill for two teas.

Clancy and his smuggling ship, of course. But how? Over the months I'd conscientiously rummaged the shabby old coaster from stem to stern, bridge to bilges: cabins, saloon, engine room, the holds, the propeller shaft. More than once I'd turned the galley inside out, hoping, for example, that the innocent-looking water-tap might spout some neat gin. But nothing. And there, standing at my elbow all the time, was Cap'n Jimmy Clancy, smiling like some innocent angel.

'A splendid and determined searcher you are, Mr Customs Man. Maybe some day, some time, you'll be coming across what you're seeking. Maybe,' Clancy once said, the usual smile still there.

'Not 'maybe', James Clancy, but 'sure certain',' I said.

'Better get your skates on, then, my friend. Now that I'm no longer throwing money away on pilotage fees I could be retiring — in, say, ten years. Listen, I'll make a promise.'

'And what'll that be?'

'The very day you pick me up I'll retire from the sea. And you can have this old ship

264

o' mine, lifeboats, compass, charts, the lot. If you ever pick me up!'

'A splendid offer, Cap'n Jim. I'll bring forward the day of reckoning as a token of my gratitude,' I said.

★ ★ ★

It was all in the course of duty. I didn't look for rewards. Every year the Dail votes me a salary and I never expect anything more. But it proved extremely difficult to refuse afternoon tea at no charge, with a deep gargle of strong mountain dew to follow, all revenues properly paid on it, of course.

I'd taken my wife for another drive along the road to Ballyragget and we'd stopped again at the country inn for afternoon tea.

Trade in liquor was now fine, the joyful publican told us, never a single drop of the hard stuff finding its illicit way inland from the coast these days. So when my wife — she's a great chatterbox — let it be known that I was the man who killed the contraband trade, the publican soared into raptures and at once conferred the freedom of the premises upon us for the rest of that day.

But I'm jumping the gun.

Clancy dropped his pilot to save a few

punts but there wasn't time to save enough to pay the fine.

Clancy's day of reckoning was one of those days when the tidal roll from the north met up with a force-nine from the south west. And they got together just outside our little harbour. From the look-out I spotted the Clancy ship, pitching and heaving and rolling like a chunk of flotsam, making, broadly, for port. Far more sensible, I thought, for Clancy to seek a steady nor'-nor'-east course and turn about as soon as the gale wore itself out. The forecast promised no more than a short, sharp blow. But not our Clancy. All of a sudden the bows of his ship swung hard aport, setting her broadside to the northerly swell of the tide. Port side awash, starboard high and dry, the coaster came scurrying over the harbour bar. And on the roll of the tide she was due, I calculated, at any moment to attack the jetty, head on.

I waited for the shuddering impact.

But there wasn't any impact. Slowly, miraculously, Clancy brought the head of his ship round and, above the roar of the gale, I heard her rusty plates scream like stuck pigs as they scraped the piles of the jetty.

I ran to examine the hull of the ship, holed and dented, fortunately well above the water line.

266

And I caught sight of the damaged rubbing strake which had struck the jetty and had rubbed for the very last time, sheered completely away by the impact.

The remnants of that rubbing strake were of particular interest to a customs officer. They showed that the strake was hollow, like a fat metal tube. And from each end there dangled a length of string.

I pulled on one of the strings and the neck of a bottle appeared. The string went on to another bottle. Then another, then another. The Clancy ship was encircled by bottles; all, I quickly discovered, containing as choice a liquor as any the publican had been experiencing intermittent difficulty in selling on the road to Ballyragget.

'You really should've kept on with the pilot, Cap'n Jim,' I called to the wheelhouse. 'Stupid to drop the man, weren't you?'

Clancy, who had seen all that I had seen, treated me to a deep, deep bellylaugh.

'Okay, Mr Customs Man, as promised, the ship's yours from now on.'

Then my ex-Cap'n Jimmy Clancy put a hand to his cheek and he bellowed, 'Ho there, below. Make it tough, make it wet for him. Open up the sea-cocks — wide, lads, wide!'

Camel of Zayid

Utterly beyond human comprehension that change in Zayid's camel. One day the most irritable and truculent beast in the whole of the Arabian desert, the next, placid and peaceful as a pet lamb.

But the change wasn't limited to a mere loss of foul temper. The powerful animal, so long the envy of every other nomad of the desert, began to jib. No matter how savagely Zayid flogged his animal, no matter how sweet the cajoling, that curious beast spurned anything more than the most reasonable of loads.

So as reasonable loads in Arabia had never yet proved economical, bankruptcy very soon was peeping at Zayid from every dip and ripple in the sand of the Arabian desert.

In a matter of weeks, Zayid's standard of living tumbled from near-affluence to a dire and grinding poverty.

At the outset Zayid was inclined to marvel at the change. So far as he knew, camels, like the sand and the sky, had never altered since time began.

Why, then, should one camel all of a

sudden begin to differ from the thousands of others that snarled and snapped their ways across the desert?

Perhaps, Zayid told himself, magic was at work. Soon, maybe, the sky would be always light, water would flow plentifully and never again would there be throats dry as wind-blown sand.

And even when his camel, in due course, became obdurate in its choice of ways across the desert, Zayid still refused to be more than a trifle anxious. The creature insisted, with an extraordinary politeness, on taking one route only from the oasis at Salwa: that well-worn track over salt-flat and sand-dune to the distant Well of Qataf. Moreover, not for Zayid's camel long hours of idleness sheltering beneath the towering Rocks of Damel. With a leer on its lips, scornful of other camels and their drivers who sought brief respite from sun and sandstorm, it dragged Zayid relentlessly onward, straight to the Well of Qataf.

Now, although this urgency earned for Zayid a desert-wide reputation for speedy deliveries from Salwa to Qataf it was also responsible for hurtling the young Arab headlong down the road to ruin. If he picked up a load for the Well there was, more often that not, a light but profitless journey back to Salwa. For the way beyond the Well of Qataf led almost to nowhere.

When abject poverty had reduced Zayid to protruding bones and frequent tears, it was beside the Well of Qataf that Zayid's strange camel found a solution to the problem of uneconomic trips back to Salwa.

With its recently developed politeness yet displaying a determination of iron, the beast refused to budge more than a few short paces away from the Well.

It might have been a most congenial existence, simply lolling beneath the palm trees that surrounded the Well of Qataf. Water was so free and plentiful that Zayid washed both himself and his camel as frequently as once a week. Food however, because Salwa lay so far from anywhere, was outrageously expensive. Zayid's only means of livelihood sprang from helping other Arabs to unload their evil-tempered camels. Here, though, earnings were comparatively trifling: Zayid had fallen badly out of practice.

From time to time there were other menial tasks for Zayid, too unpleasant to relate, so that he might keep himself and his lazy camel holding on to life. Yet the beast was never more than mildly appreciative of Zayid's efforts. Offered the most toothsome titbit the creature barely blinked an eye. Yet, whenever some stranger came to the Well of Qataf, the camel would at once lurch to its feet for a detailed inspection of the new arrival. But reaction was always the same: the shake of the head, a slight curl of ugly lips, the settling down once more at the feet of its wondering master.

Like his body, however, Zayid's wonderment began to grow exceedingly thin. No longer was he feeling any excitement over the mystery of his camel. There were times when patience was skinnier even than wonderment. But the kicks aimed at the camel's protruding ribs, urging a return to Salwa, proved less than useless.

In spite of the agony, the animal remained friendly and not in the least resentful. But it also remained as motionless and solid as the ancient rocks of Damel.

Without food to accompany it, the water from the Well of Qataf had long since taken on a brackish flavour. The day arrived when Zayid, who had not eaten for a week, became light-headed, desperate. Begging, beating and kicking had all failed. With considerable reluctance Zayid decided to sell his camel. Even a donkey, he thought, with only one tenth of the carrying capacity of a normal, truculent camel, would be a far superior investment. Indeed, on present

271

showing, any kind of donkey, no matter how decrepit, would be more productive than his motionless, sweet-tempered creature.

But there was no queue of potential customers clamouring for a camel that had been idling beside the Well of Qataf for months on end. Not one of the hundreds of nomads who came weekly to the well was in the least interested. They were amused, of course. The story of the man who performed all manner of menial tasks simply to support a weary camel had been embroidered and spread the length and breadth of the Arabian desert.

'Not for me, Zayid. If you wish to sell me a camel then sell me one that will work for its living.'

'Ah, but deep in the heart of my camel there lies a great secret. Uncover that secret and then he will work like ten camels, I promise you.'

'You could well be right, Zayid. Your camel, indeed, holds a truly wonderful secret. And if you do not take care it could spread like some foul pestilence to every other camel in the desert. It's the only beast in the whole of Arabia that knows how to put a man to work to keep sit-down camels in bone-idle luxury.'

Many a day and many a night of rumbling, empty bellies had staggered by when, one evening, a negro arrived, limping, at the Well of Qataf. Hands clasped about his knees, head down, Zayid ignored the approach of the man but his camel glanced up with a lively interest.

'Is that the camel you've got for sale?' the negro said.

Zayid nodded and rose. His camel was already on its feet.

'And very cheap, it is. The price of three donkeys, that's all.'

'Three very ancient donkeys, maybe,' the negro said, as he walked round the camel, deftly poking between the creature's protruding bones.

'But he's a wonderful camel, finest desert breed,' Zayid said, struggling meantime to conceal with his hands widespread the scrawny frame. 'If you're in a great hurry, though, I could let him go for the price of two good donkeys.'

'I certainly am in a great hurry,' the negro replied, 'but not in such a hurry as all that.'

'Then — then I might let him go for just one and a half very good donkeys.'

273

The traveller glanced at his bare feet, swollen, bleeding, blistered.

'For the price of one and a half then,' he said.

The camel, ears sharply cocked over the bargaining, nosed Zayid away and sniffed at the negro appreciatively.

The trio sat down together and, after settling the account, the customer shared his meagre stock of food with Zayid and the camel.

As night fell, the man stood up and the camel, although in a deep and peaceful sleep, at once lurched to its feet.

Zayid was weak, the negro still weary. There were ten minutes of feverish struggle before Zayid managed to hoist his customer to the camel's back. Beneath its unaccustomed burden, the creature sagged so that its belly was almost touching the sand yet there was no evident sign of resentment.

As the pair swept off into the darkness Zayid heaved a sigh of relief.

'Dirt cheap at the price,' he called. 'I made no charge for my camel's wonderful secret, remember!'

Scarcely had Zayid settled down to count the negro's money again and to consider donkey loads when huge wet lips began to caress the back of his neck. The camel drew up its legs and settled down beside him once more.

Minutes later the negro came stumbling back to the Well.

'Hands off my money. That camel of yours is a fraud. And you're no better yourself!'

Dropping to his knees, the man scooped up the coins that had been standing in neat piles on the sand of Qataf.

Zayid stared open-mouthed.

'But — but what's — what's been happening?'

'Happening? You know well enough, Arab, what's been happening. Barely a thousand paces on the way to Salwa and that beast of yours pitched me over its head.'

'On the way to Salwa? But I explained, didn't I? My camel never had the slightest fancy for the Salwa direction.'

'Hm!!'

Snatching up the remaining coins, the negro aimed a savage kick at Zayid's placid beast then went off in search of more reliable transport.

For once no longer hungry yet bone-grinding cold, Zayid drew tattered cloak about skinny shoulders and, the camel lying beside him, he fell asleep.

The night was bright with a million stars but none so bright as Zayid's dreams.

Tall, rich men in flowing velvet cloaks were offering whole strings of fat, young donkeys just for the price of one lazy, lolling camel. But not for one hundred strings was Zayid willing to sell. Locked up in his camel there lay a valuable secret. Two hundred strings then? No, not even five hundred!

Zayid awoke with a start.

Astride a donkey, a cloaked and hooded stranger, black against the night sky, was approaching. The camel lurched to its feet and shambled towards the newcomer.

'Peace to you and yours!' the stranger said from the depths of his hood.

'Peace it is,' the shivering Zayid said as he laid hold of his camel's rope.

'An extremely fine beast you have there,' the man said as he threw back hood and cloak to reveal a dusky countenance and richly embroidered garments.

Dragging at its rope, the camel struggled hard to nuzzle the dark and bearded face.

'Back, back, useless one,' Zayid said. 'Back to your dreams and your bone-idleness!'

'No, no! Permit him to come,' the stranger said as he stroked the camel's snout. 'See, he takes a great fancy to me. I knew he would, of course.'

Zayid looked puzzled.

'You — you knew he would! How could you possibly know such a thing?!!'

The stranger dismounted from his donkey.

'An animal of little use, you say? Well I could make substantial use of him, my friend. This donkey is now slow and weary. I must have a camel, long-legged and swift. Will you sell?'

Zayid was hesitant.

'Are you by any chance heading in the direction of Salwa?'

'No, no, not Salwa. The other way entirely. Come, take my donkey in exchange. After a few days' rest, he will be capable of carrying you to the ends of the earth if needs be. You will find him an earnest and devoted servant. And if my donkey is not sufficient there is gold as well.'

The stranger held out a handful of coins.

Zayid was still hesitant. He was seeking no repetition of the last selling fiasco. The negro had been feeble and scrawny. This newcomer was large and powerful. If the wretched camel again changed its mind after a thousand paces into the desert, the man might return to murder them both.

'I — don't — quite — know,' he said.

The stranger flung his handful of coins to the ground and quickly followed with a second handful.

'Name your figure. The donkey may be weak but my gold is strong enough!'

'I — I'd like to — very much!' Zayid said.

'Quickly, quickly make up your mind. My time grows desperately short. Within minutes I must be on my way.'

'But not to Salwa, sir?'

'Not to Salwa, I tell you!'

Zayid's eyes were on more gold coins flung to the sand. He remembered the brackish water, the rumbling belly and the icy nights by the Well of Qataf.

'My camel is yours!' he said.

'Splendid!'

At once the stranger leapt to the camel's back.

In a cloud of dust the pair swung swiftly away from the Well of Qataf, away from the direction of Salwa, away into the black velvet unknown of the Arabian night.

As they sped like the wind over the desert sand Zayid watched in wonderment. Far to the north-west of the galloping pair he saw a Great Star coursing its way across the heavens.

The secret of Zayid's camel was still a secret from Zayid.

But his camel knew. It had known all along.

With Balthasar and Melchior, Caspar, dark-skinned king of Ethiopia, would now be in plenty of time to pay his homage to another King who lay in a manger in the distant Judaean town of Bethlehem.

McLEAN AT THE GOLDEN OWL
George Goodchild
Inspector McLean has resigned from Scotland Yard's CID and has opened an office in Wimpole Street. With the help of his able assistant, Tiny, he solves many crimes, including those of kidnapping, murder and poisoning.

KATE WEATHERBY
Anne Goring
Derbyshire, 1849: The Hunter family are the arrogant, powerful masters of Clough Grange. Their feuds are sparked by a generation of guilt, despair and ill-fortune. But their passions are awakened by the arrival of nineteen-year-old Kate Weatherby.

A VENETIAN RECKONING
Donna Leon
When the body of a prominent international lawyer is found in the carriage of an intercity train, Commissario Guido Brunetti begins to dig deeper into the secret lives of the once great and good.

A TASTE FOR DEATH
Peter O'Donnell

Modesty Blaise and Willie Garvin take on impossible odds in the shape of Simon Delicata, the man with a taste for death, and Swordmaster, Wenczel, in a terrifying duel. Finally, in the Sahara desert, the intrepid pair must summon every killing skill to survive.

SEVEN DAYS FROM MIDNIGHT
Rona Randall

In the Comet Theatre, London, seven people have good reason for wanting beautiful Maxine Culver out of the way. Each one has reason to fear her blackmail. But whose shadow is it that lurks in the wings, waiting to silence her once and for all?

QUEEN OF THE ELEPHANTS
Mark Shand

Mark Shand knows about the ways of elephants, but he is no match for the tiny Parbati Barua, the daughter of India's greatest expert on the Asian elephant, the late Prince of Gauripur, who taught her everything. Shand sought out Parbati to take part in a film about the plight of the wild herds today in north-east India.

THE DARKENING LEAF
Caroline Stickland

On storm-tossed Chesil Bank in 1847, the young lovers, Philobeth and Frederick, prevent wreckers mutilating the apparent corpse of a young woman. Discovering she is still alive, Frederick takes her to his grandmother's home. But the rescue is to have violent and far-reaching effects . . .

A WOMAN'S TOUCH
Emma Stirling

When Fenn went to stay on her uncle's farm in Africa, the lovely Helena Starr seemed to resent her — especially when Dr Jason Kemp agreed to Fenn helping in his bush hospital. Though it seemed Jason saw Fenn as little more than a child, her feelings for him were those of a woman.

A DEAD GIVEAWAY
Various Authors

This book offers the perfect opportunity to sample the skills of five of the finest writers of crime fiction — Clare Curzon, Gillian Linscott, Peter Lovesey, Dorothy Simpson and Margaret Yorke.

DOUBLE INDEMNITY — MURDER FOR INSURANCE
Jad Adams

This is a collection of true cases of murderers who insured their victims then killed them — or attempted to. Each tense, compelling account tells a story of cold-blooded plotting and elaborate deception.

THE PEARLS OF COROMANDEL
By Keron Bhattacharya

John Sugden, an ambitious young Oxford graduate, joins the Indian Civil Service in the early 1920s and goes to uphold the British Raj. But he falls in love with a young Hindu girl and finds his loyalties tragically divided.

WHITE HARVEST
Louis Charbonneau

Kathy McNeely, a marine biologist, sets out for Alaska to carry out important research. But when she stumbles upon an illegal ivory poaching operation that is threatening the world's walrus population, she soon realises that she will have to survive more than the harsh elements . . .

TO THE GARDEN ALONE
Eve Ebbett

Widow Frances Morley's short, happy marriage was childless, and in a succession of borders she attempts to build a substitute relationship for the husband and family she does not have. Over all hovers the shadow of the man who terrorized her childhood.

CONTRASTS
Rowan Edwards

Julia had her life beautifully planned — she was building a thriving pottery business as well as sharing her home with her friend Pippa, and having fun owning a goat. But the goat's problems brought the new local vet, Sebastian Trent, into their lives.

MY OLD MAN AND THE SEA
David and Daniel Hays

Some fathers and sons go fishing together. David and Daniel Hays decided to sail a tiny boat seventeen thousand miles to the bottom of the world and back. Together, they weave a story of travel, adventure, and difficult, sometimes terrifying, sailing.

SQUEAKY CLEAN
James Pattinson

An important attribute of a prospective candidate for the United States presidency is not to have any dirt in your background which an eager muckraker can dig up. Senator William S. Gallicauder appeared to fit the bill perfectly. But then a skeleton came rattling out of an English cupboard.

NIGHT MOVES
Alan Scholefield

It was the first case that Macrae and Silver had worked on together. Malcolm Underdown had brutally stabbed to death Edward Craig and had attempted to murder Craig's fiancée, Jane Harrison. He swore he would be back for her. Now, four years later, he has simply walked from the mental hospital. Macrae and Silver must get to him — before he gets to Jane.

GREATEST CAT STORIES
Various Authors

Each story in this collection is chosen to show the cat at its best. James Herriot relates a tale about two of his cats. Stella Whitelaw has written a very funny story about a lion. Other stories provide examples of courageous, clever and lucky cats.

THE HAND OF DEATH
Margaret Yorke

The woman had been raped and murdered. As the police pursue their relentless inquiries, decent, gentle George Fortescue, the typical man-next-door, finds himself accused. While the real killer serenely selects his third victim — and then his fourth . . .

VOW OF FIDELITY
Veronica Black

Sister Joan of the Daughters of Compassion is shocked to discover that three of her former fellow art college students have recently died violently. When another death occurs, Sister Joan realizes that she must pit her wits against a cunning and ruthless killer.

MARY'S CHILD
Irene Carr

Penniless and desperate, Chrissie struggles to support herself as the Victorian years give way to the First World War. Her childhood friends, Ted and Frank, fall hopelessly in love with her. But there is only one man Chrissie loves, and fate and one man bent on revenge are determined to prevent the match . . .

THE SWIFTEST EAGLE
Alice Dwyer-Joyce

This book moves from Scotland to Malaya — before British Raj and now — and then to war-torn Vietnam and Cambodia . . . Virginia meets Gareth casually in the Western Isles, with no inkling of the sacrifice he must make for her.

VICTORIA & ALBERT
Richard Hough

Victoria and Albert had nine children and the family became the archetype of the nineteenth century. But the relationship between the Queen and her Prince Consort was passionate and turbulent; thunderous rows threatened to tear them apart, but always reconciliation and love broke through.

BREEZE: WAIF OF THE WILD
Marie Kelly

Bernard and Marie Kelly swapped their lives in London for a remote farmhouse in Cumbria. But they were to undergo an even more drastic upheaval when a two-day-old fragile roe deer fawn arrived on their doorstep. The knowledge of how to care for her was learned through sleepless nights and anxiety-filled days.

DEAR LAURA
Jean Stubbs
In Victorian London, Mr Theodore Crozier, of Crozier's Toys, succumbed to three grains of morphine. Wimbledon hoped it was suicide — but murder was whispered. Out of the neat cupboards of the Croziers' respectable home tumbled skeleton after skeleton.

MOTHER LOVE
Judith Henry Wall
Karen Billingsly begins to suspect that her son, Chad, has done something unthinkable — something beyond her wildest fears or imaginings. Gradually the terrible truth unfolds, and Karen must decide just how far she should go to protect her son from justice.

JOURNEY TO GUYANA
Margaret Bacon
In celebration of the anniversary of the emancipation of the African slaves in Guyana, the author published an account of her two-year stay there in the 1960s, revealing some fascinating insights into the multi-racial society.

WEDDING NIGHT
Gary Devon

Young actress Callie McKenna believes that Malcolm Rhodes is the man of her dreams. But a dark secret long buried in Malcolm's past is about to turn Callie's passion into terror.

RALPH EDWARDS
OF LONESOME LAKE
Ed Gould

Best known for his almost single-handed rescue of the trumpeter swans from extinction in North America, Ralph Edwards relates other aspects of his long, varied life, including experiences with his missionary parents in India, as a telegraph operator in World War I, and his eventual return to Lonesome Lake.

NEVER FAR FROM NOWHERE
Andrea Levy

Olive and Vivien were born in London to Jamaican parents. Vivien's life becomes a chaotic mix of friendships, youth clubs, skinhead violence, discos and college. But Olive, three years older and her skin a shade darker, has a very different tale to tell . . .